Showtime 2023

The Collected Works of Newham Writers

Copyright © 2023 by Newham Writers Workshop and the respective authors.

ISBN: 9798859513574

All rights reserved. No part of this publication may be reproduced, distributed, or transmitted in any form or by any means, including photocopying, recording or other electronic or mechanical methods, without the prior written permission of the publisher and the authors, except in the case of brief quotations embodied in critical reviews and certain other non-commercial uses permitted by copyright law.

www.newhamwriters.wordpress.com

Front Cover: Alphabetti Spaghetti Alex Chinneck, Canning Town, East London,
Photograph by Martin Peache,
    his Instagram:
    https://www.instagram.com/martinpeache/.

Published by Newham Writers Workshop.

Contents   Page

Introduction: Welcome to a new anthology   6
Noise: a poem by Paul Butler   7
Confessions of a Black Cab Driver:
    a non-fiction essay by Jeff Jones   14
Alfie: a poem by Mandy Grainger   25
Just Looking:
    a poem by Andrew Diamond   26
The House That No-One Built:
    a short story by Belgin Durmush   27
Beautiful-Words: a poem by Deborah Collins   38
Even a Monkey Can Fall from a Tree:
    a short story by Drew Payne   40
Safe Space: a poem by Frances Ogiemwense   63
In The Rose Garden: a short story by Dharma Paul   64
You'll Have to Make do With Me: a poem by Frank Crocker   67
Time Grinds to a Halt in the Coffee Shop:
    a short story by Sarah Winslow   69
The Forgotten Tree: a poem by Shah Obaid   71
Me and My Shadow: a short story by Rob Masson   72
The Tankard's Mahogany Bar: a poem by George Fuller   82
The Tulip Thesis: a short story by Michael Frank   87
Days Like These: a poem by Frances Ogiemwense   97
Uncle Bob: a non-fiction essay by Dave Chambers   98
Resignation: a poem by Catherine Daniels   105
Mission to Zelba: a short story by Paul Germain   106
On the Central Line: a poem by Andrew Diamond   110

More Tales of Glo and Laura: a short story by Ros Allison	111
A Thousand Tongues: a poem by Mark Altenor	120
A Southern Aspect: a short story by Nicola Catton	121
Driving to Work with a Stowaway: a poem by Mandy Grainger	124
The Worst of Times Part 1:	
a non-fiction essay by Frank Crocker	126
Eco Friendly: a poem by George Fuller	132
Customer Service: a short story by Michael Frank	134
A Run around Mount Tamapalais:	
a poem by Frances Ogiemwense	143
In The Café: a poem by George Fuller	144
Farewell: a short story by Shah Obaid	146
Misspent Youth: a poem by Mandy Grainger	152
Grandma: a poem by Andrew Diamond	153
Margaret Griffith, In Praise of Librarians:	
a memorial essay about our former treasurer	155
Authors' Bios	158
Afterword	168

Welcome to a new anthology of writing from East London

We are a creative writing workshop catering for adults who write or would like to write factual or fictional literary works. It has been another eventful year with many inspiring and thoughtful pieces read in the workshop over the course of the year with the aim of developing creative and technical skills and receiving constructive feedback in the process.

This year's anthology is filled with wonderful contributions of poetry, prose, fiction, science fiction, as well as non-fiction; with deliberations on grief, love, friendship, religion and much, much more.

Members get their inspiration from many places such as a trip down memory lane or an imagined meeting with their hero; or an everyday event that is turned into a stream of consciousness for the reader. Whatever the inspiration, this creates a rich mixture of talent within the workshop for us all to enjoy.

Plunge into the thoughts and ideas shared in this anthology and enjoy the selection of inventive, mad, moving and sometimes disturbing pieces put together by members who continue to thrive with the support of our workshop.

Belgin Durmush, Ros Allison & Drew Payne
(The editorial team)

Noise by Paul Butler

Mr Williams has anxiety

No idea why

You really must improve Mr Williams

Relax better Mr Williams

Take the day as it comes Mr Williams

Go with the flow Mr Williams

It's a journey

Not a destination

Live the moment

Now Mr Williams

Just take a few minutes each day to …

      Count your calories

      Count your veg

      Count your fruit

      Check it's trade fair

      Check it's green

      Check it's wage fair

      Sustainable

      Organic

      And your yoghurt is probiotic

      Cholesterol reducing

      Gut enhancing

      Measure your waist

Your hips

Your BMI

Go vegan

But eat your fish

Eat your oats

Eat your tofu

And be careful where you buy.

Meditate

Every day

Be mindful

Every day

Journal

Every day

Only takes a minute or two

Then go within

To find yourself

Then go without

To fast

Seize the day

Use the hour

Cherish the moment

Live each day as if it were your…

But become aware

Become at one

Stay in the now

But look to the future

Hear your inner voice

But close that voice in your head

Then open your chakras

Open your mind

Be true to yourself

But face your unconscious bias

Mr Williams you really could be a better version of…

You can be anything you want to be

So be the change you want to see

It's all down to you, you see

But love yourself as you are

Chant you are perfect

Chant you're enough

Mantra you're worthy

Chant you're a star

Know you're blessed

Repeat you are loved

It only takes a minute or two

Then go find your life.

Oh and do try to shine

And strengthen your core

Every day

Tighten your glutes

Every day

Your abs

Biceps

Triceps

Walk 10,000 steps

But lower your carbon footprint

Lower your blood pressure

Lower your screen time

Lower your cholesterol

Lower your spending

Lower your calories

Lower your sugars

Lower your booze

Lower your salt

Every day

And lose ten pounds

Swim

Cycle

Recycle

And re-swim ... oops sorry that's daft ... lots to remember.

Pray

Every day

Then stretch

Every day

Just takes ten minutes

Pilates

Yoga

Core

Gratitude training

Every day

Spiritual awakening

Every day

Make down time

But give it your all

To follow your dream

To do your best

Then go with the flow

And flow with your breaths

And breathe with your soul

You'll reap what you sow

So listen and grow

And glo up

And study

And learn

And unlearn

But do get some fresh air

And for heaven's sake chill.

Take a holiday

Oh but do be green

Save for your future

But please give generously

Count your privilege

But do recount your misfortunes

…in a professional setting of course

Let it all out

To let love in

And make sure you get closure

And don't forget to floss.

And declutter

And detox

But stay hydrated

And don't go in the sun

And take screen breaks

Dear me that posture

Get your eyes checked

And your ears

Have you checked your moles?

Dress up to date

But don't follow fashion

And love yourself

And love your look

And know your worth

You're fine as you are

So go change yourself

Change your life

Change your passwords

Change your vibes

Change those bulbs

And check your prostate.

Then you can start each day Mr Williams
And become
Our ideal version of you.

Oh Tut Tut Mr Williams.

Mr Williams has anxiety

No idea why.

Confessions of a Black Cab driver by Jeff Jones

1 My Hero

I've been a London Black Taxi driver since 2014 after a career as a manager in youth work and mental health. Some of the passengers I've recognised were household names and others I've discovered were famous during conversation. As a rule, when customers enter my taxi, I confirm their destination, followed by a polite flurry of small talk, such as the weather, before turning my microphone off, the radio up and continuing on the journey. I never intrude on their privacy as I respect that they may want to engage on their phone, travel in silence or converse with the company they may be with.

However, there are times when I turn my mic back on when the passenger wants to talk to me, which I never have a problem with as I see it as an opportunity to gain knowledge and ask questions to people I never usually meet. There are times when customers are very open and honest, from multi-millionaire bankers/company directors, soldiers, explorers, actors, footballers and people from all walks of life.

About 3pm, one Wednesday afternoon, October 2022, I accepted a job on an app to pick up at a restaurant in Smithfield Market, going to Waterloo Station. I approached the restaurant and there stood a man in his 60's with silver hair waving his arm. As I stopped, to my astonishment I recognized him to be Gary Lineker, the football icon, and one of my idols who I tried to emulate on the football pitch many times.

I stopped, opened the window and said, "alright Gary," as though I knew him personally.

With a smile, he said, "hello. Waterloo please," and got into the taxi. Due to trying to process this encounter as I was overwhelmed, I didn't try any small talk like I usually did. There I had my idol Gary Lineker sitting in my cab, the prolific Centre Forward who played for Leicester, Tottenham, Everton, England, Barcelona, and won the Golden Boot in a World Cup finals. The taxi was in silence while I listened to LBC on the radio.

Coincidently, the topic being discussed on LBC was the World Cup being hosted in Qatar in two months' time, and whether or not it should be boycotted due to the attitude of the host nation towards the LGBTQ community. After a few minutes, I checked in the mirror and noticed that Gary wasn't engaged on his phone, he was just looking out of the window. I broke the silence and asked, "Gary are you going to Qatar?"

"Yes, I'll be working there. It should be a good tournament."

"What do you think of England's chances of winning?"

"Well, obviously, I'd like them to do well, and although they showed a lot of promise in the Euros, losing on penalties in the final, I think that Brazil or Argentina will win it."

"I've always followed football, and played, and reached semi-pro standard, and as we're similar ages I grew up watching you play. You were quick over 2 to 20 yards."

"2 to 20 yards! I was quick over 100 yards."

"Ok, what comes to mind is your quick darting runs in the box and playing off of the shoulder of defenders."

"Yes, I did that as well."

"Mind you, you had the privilege of playing in a World Cup. Wow!! What an experience."

"I've actually played in two World Cups."

"Oh! Of course you have. And you also won the Golden Boot, and played against one the greatest players ever, Maradona, at the time when he claimed his goal was from the hand of God."

"Maradona, undoubtedly was the best player I've played against. I was too far away from the incident but I knew it was a hand ball from the reaction of our players who were closer to him."

"That second goal Maradona scored was one of the best goals I've ever seen. He took on half of the England team and had the composure to take the ball around Peter Shilton before putting it into the net. It doesn't matter how many times I see that goal I always find it breathtaking."

"Yes, that goal was phenomenal. I remember just standing there, mesmerized, hoping he'd be tackled. It was such a great goal I had to stop myself from applauding," Gary laughed.

"Who was the best player you ever played with, Gary?"

"Without a doubt, Peter Beardsley. He did pretty much all the hard work and I had the easy job of making the runs in the box."

I pulled up outside of Waterloo Station.

"It was nice talking to you, Gary."

"Likewise, bye," he said, as he slammed the door shut.

As Gary Lineker walked away I thought to myself, why didn't I ask him for a selfie?

If I was asked what living person I would like to meet, before I met Gary Lineker, I would have probably chosen to meet him. As not only did I admire Gary as a footballer growing up, as he was a great striker, he was also a fair player who was never booked or sent off during his career. Gary Lineker achieved so much, both in and out of the game, and is now a successful football pundit and speaks out on his political beliefs despite being attacked by the right wing media. This, I also admire, as Gary could have kept quiet

and just lived a charmed life rather than put himself into the firing line. Most of what Gary stands up for, I agree with. I feel privileged to have met one of my idols and speaking with him was easy as he was so enthusiastic to engage in dialog. In my opinion, Gary Lineker is one of the greatest Englishman of my generation.

2 The Trail Blazer

I sat at the taxi rank at Paddington Station, this sunny July afternoon, moving slowly towards the swarm of passengers, who in turn were shuffling into the cab at the front. I was now second in line, as the taxi in front of me pulled away, I turned my light off to 'hired' as a black gentleman walked towards me, speaking on his phone. I said to myself, "that's John Barnes." As he got to the front window that was open I said, "Barnsey."

"Alright? I want to go to 241 Great Portland Street and on to Euston Station please." He held his hand over the phone.

"Ok John, jump in mate."

As John was speaking on the phone, I was processing the moment. Wow, I have John Barnes in my taxi, the trail blazer, the ex-Watford, Liverpool and England winger! What a player he was. John came off the phone. I waited a while and said, "how are you, John?"

"Good, thanks. Once we get to Great Portland Street I'd like you to wait a while for me before going to Euston."

"Yes, Ok. John I remember seeing you once at a football related function in Windsor a few years ago."

"Oh, yes. What was you doing there, did you play?"

"Yes, semi-professionally, but I knew a premier league player that allowed me access to the event. We're similar in age so I followed you throughout your career. Did you find it hard to retire from the game?"

"Yes, in some ways, the routine and the banter with the other players. One thing that I didn't miss was the training. Besides, I stayed involved in the game in management and played football for fun when I could."

"It's that restaurant that you want there on the left John."

"Yes. Please wait, I'll be 10 minutes."

"Ok, I'm going to trust you, so don't do a runner," I joked. John smirked and got out.

Minutes later....

Jumping in and slamming the taxi door. "Now on to Euston please."

"John, who was the best players you ever played with?"

"Oh that's easy. Ian Rush and Alan Hansen."

"How about Kenny Dalglish? I thought he would have been up there?"

"No, I didn't play with Kenny. He signed me as Liverpool manager."

"Oh, of course, he played before you. Dalglish was a great player. He could turn on a sixpence. I used to watch West Ham play as they are my local team but I'm not patriotic and I can appreciate good players, and Ian Rush was deadly in front of goal. What a striker!"

"Rushy was always reliable."

As we approached Euston station...

"I need to run to catch my train, so don't go into the station as there's a long queue of traffic, so let me off here please. How much do I owe you?"

"£32.00 please."

"Here's forty. Keep the change."

"Thanks John. Can I have a selfie with you?"

"Yes, make it quick." I jumped out of the cab posing next to John with my phone in front of our face. It was then that I realized that I had never taken a selfie before and as I fiddled with the phone John said, "give us it here," took the phone from me and took a few snaps.

"Thanks John. It was nice meeting you."

"Take care." John ran off towards the station.

John Barnes was an idol of mine, growing up, as he was exciting to watch and he got people off of their seats with his skills and scoring goals. I also admired John's courage and attitude playing during a time when racism on the terraces was rife and vocal. I recall an incident when John went to take a corner kick as some of the crowd aimed bananas at him. John peeled a banana, ate it, and took the corner. John Barnes scored the best goal I have ever seen from a player in an England shirt. England were playing Brazil in a friendly, and John received the ball on the left, thirty-five yards from the goal, and ran at the Brazilian defence, dribbling past about six players before putting the ball into the net. It was a goal you expect to be scored by the Brazilian team and not by England.

John Barnes MBE, is often considered as one of the greatest English players of all time and currently works as a football pundit and commentator. John is also an author, writing a book 'The Uncomfortable Truth About Racism', and is considered an ambassador, delivering many talks and participating in discussions.

Although I feel fortunate to have meet John Barnes I don't get 'star struck' as I think that's because I have experienced being among top footballers and as a result I don't get over-excited. Besides, in my trade, I have to behave professionally, and, after all, they're just passengers like anyone else. It's only my passion for football that drives me to engage in dialog with players. There are times when I recognize famous people in my taxi that I don't attempt to have a conversation with, as I'm not interested in what they do. However, I always acknowledge them at the end of the journey.

3 Road Rage

I was in my taxi driving Eastbound on the Marylebone Road, when I noticed the driver of a red electric taxi in front of me and a cyclist peddling alongside, arguing with each other. As we approached the red traffic lights, the cyclist veered off to the third lane and stopped at the lights, as did the red taxi, with me pulling up behind. The pair of them continued shouting at each other as I turned my radio down and opened the window to try to hear what their beef was about. The cyclist did a U-turn on his bike, riding the wrong way down lane one, and with his right leg kicked the red taxi. The driver flew out of his cab, grabbing the cyclist's collar with both hands. The cyclist then punched him in the face causing the cabbie's nose to bleed. The incident took place a couple of feet next to me. The cabbie shouted, "someone call the police," whilst frog-marching the cyclist, who had been sitting on his bike, to the pavement next to my taxi.

I phoned the police and explained what I had witnessed and our location, and I was told by the operator that as it was an emergency, the police would be with me soon. I jumped out of my taxi to support the cabbie as he was the victim, and to try to defuse the situation. The taxi driver was a white male, 5'10, about 40 years old, stocky build, and the cyclist looked Mediterranean about 6 foot and slim build, about 40 years old.

The cabbie was still holding on to the cyclist who was shouting, "let me go," and struggling. His bike was now against the wall.

I approached them, and said, "I've called the police, they're on their way." I turned to the cyclist. "Do yourself a favour and calm down and wait for the police."

He stopped struggling and said, "he started it! Did you hear what he said to me?"

"No, I didn't. The thing is you went too far when you had the opportunity to ride away at the traffic lights but you didn't. I saw you U-turn and kick his £72,000 cab, and then punch him in the face. You have no argument, so shut up and wait for the police, and don't you dare hit him again."

"Ok, can I wait in your taxi?"

"No, wait here. The police won't be long."

Suddenly a huge white bloke about 35 years old and 6'5 tall, stopped and said to the cyclist, "you fucking punched him, you fucking foreigner. You shouldn't even be in this fucking country."

The cyclist, who was still being collared by the cabbie, replied, "you're being racist now," and took out his phone and started filming the passer-by.

"I don't give a fuck, you fucking foreigner. You're lucky coz you punched him and not me, as you would be on the fucking deck, knocked out cold."

"Go on, continue. I've got you on film," screamed the cyclist, whilst the passer-by continued with a barrage of racist abuse.

My mind totally switched off at that point, feeling confused and thinking, 'I'm trying to help the cabbie, and me being black, this bloke is hurling racial abuse. Hasn't he any manners?' I stood between them both and said, "Look mate, just go, you're only making matters worse." The passer-by then knocked the phone out of the cyclist's hands and walked off. As the cyclist picked his phone off the ground, I said, "Just keep calm and wait for the police as there's nothing more to discuss, Ok."

"The police are going to look at him more favourable as he is a local and I am not," said the cyclist, pointing at the cabbie.

"The sooner you accept your responsibility the better, as you're to blame. If he jumped out of his cab and attacked you like you did to him, I would be defending you. I'm not defending him just because he's a cabbie like myself. So don't come with that nonsense."

A few minutes later, two police cars with their sirens on pulled up, and out jumped six police officers and surrounded us. The cabbie said, "can I let go now?"

"Yes, it's Ok now," said an officer. Two police officers each, separated the three of us and questioned us on what had happened.

The cabbie, with blood still streaming from his nose, asked an officer, "have you any tissues please?"

I said, "I have," and gave the cabbie some tissues and wet wipes that I took from my taxi.

The cabbie wiped the blood from his face, looked at his cab and said to the police, "yes there's a dent on the door where he kicked it."

I told the police exactly what I had witnessed and gave a statement. An hour later I was told I could leave and that I'd be contacted when it went to court or for any further information. As I walked to my taxi, the cabbie got out of the back of his taxi where he was giving a statement, shook my hand and said, "I'm Joe. Thanks for stopping. There's not many people who would have done that."

"I'm Jeff. That's Ok. If it goes to court, I'll be there." I left the scene. There was no sign of the cyclist. He was probably arrested for criminal damage and assault.

I called my wife Gloria and explained to her what had happened.

"Jeff you're 61 years old. In your mind, you may think that you can still handle yourself, but that cyclist was 20 years younger than you. He was desperate and cornered like a wild animal. What if he pulled out a knife?"

"I reacted instinctively, and didn't think of the consequences. However, you have got a point as I am getting on, and the cyclist could have pulled out
a knife and the outcome could have been so different, who's to know?"

"Besides, out of all those cars that were at the traffic lights at the time of the incident who else stopped? No-one. And why do you think that was?"

"I get your point," I replied, "and I will take it on board if something like this happens in future."

On reflection, I reacted totally on instinct as you can never predict what you'll find in a situation like this. I think due to my experience of working as a manager in Youth and Community Work for many years, and having to deal with conflict resolution, I was able to defuse the situation successfully. However, thankfully, there was a positive outcome.

"What use is a lion without any teeth?"

Alfie by Mandy Grainger

Let me tell you about the happiest chap
With a dapper coat of white and black
Who strolled the block and with a broad smile,
Greeted every face within a quarter-mile

With charming swagger and his air easy,
He offered his mousing services freely
And for a scratch on the ear or a kind word
He'd give you the most impressive purr

And often with his pink nose twitching
He knew what lurked within your kitchen
Such were his manners that he never begged,
But I think he had every soft heart pegged

On warm days, he sunned on a patio step
On cold days, we'd wonder where he slept
Yet a few days later, you would get a sense
Of a grey-tipped tail flicking by the fence

Well, clouds have cleared now; the sun shines again
But I am sad to say that our whiskered friend
Has found himself a new place to sleep
Where the warmth is plenty, and dreams are deep

Just Looking by Andrew Diamond

Don't stare, stop looking at me
Encroaching on my privacy.
Your eyes are chiselling at my face;
Avert your gaze, look into space.
How dare you glare at me like that.
Oh what the hell, you're just a cat!

The House That No-one Built by Belgin Durmush

It appeared, suddenly, the house that no-one built, peering like a black flower over the wilderness above their wooden shack. It stood, magnificent and dreary on the hilltop where the oak tree, torn down by the great storm, used to stand. Muriel stared at it from her window. In all these years, the house had never seemed so close. In all these years she had kept its existence hidden, even from herself, for what good were her visions of doom to anybody? But now, there it stood, as if emerging from her dreams.

She didn't tell Lucy. Not immediately. It was better to wait. And so she waited, day after day, checking the window for signs of sky, wringing her hands under her apron so Lucy would not see. She shifted uncomfortably on her stool in the pantry, the only dry place left in the shack, and looked at Lucy. Could Lucy not see the house on the hill? She dared not ask, afraid of what she might say. Mad doolally woman! Unhinged like a pipped fruit! Go back to your mad world and leave the sane be. Or maybe she would cry, a look of concern creeping into her face that Muriel wouldn't be able to bear. Have you finally flipped? Lucy would say, and the pain would consume her face.

Muriel pressed her forehead to the window, pretending to inspect the grit in her worn fingernails. She didn't want to worry Lucy. Lucy was too frail for worries: her head in her book, a slight smile on her lips. She didn't tell her how the house planted from a seed in her dreams seemed to be watching her. And so she sat there, listening to its whispers whistling through the window, her skin crawling like the grave itself was calling her:

>Your time has come,
>
>Your days are done,
>
>Stand by the house you built,

Little fruit.

The words rang and rang, and she sat up straight in her chair, like a rake, stiff and unyielding, as if to awaken her old bones to the strange prickling sounds. She looked at the old tree that too had yielded to the unknown and the unknowable, now lying dormant at the top of the hill, and then again at Lucy, an innocent despite her years, head down, flour and tinned food stacked high where she sat as if to fortify her. What could she do about poor Lucy? She gazed back at the hilltop and the towering majesty of degradation that crowned it like despair itself, her own cold body lying beside the tree like an omen. She twitched with the sight, barely able to conceal the nerves running through her tired old body. Her trembling hand flew to her face and her mouth was dry as she turned to Lucy, whose head was still inside the book she was reading by the dimming light of the window.

"Lucy, dear, I want you to do something for me."

"What is it, Muriel, dear?"

"Look out of the window and tell me what you see."

Lucy put her book down on her lap, carefully folded her glasses and stared outside.

"The street. The farmhouse just ahead. The hillside. And rain. Will it ever stop?"

"Yes, yes, yes, but look where the tree used to be."

"Ah, yes. That poor tree. What a pity it is dead." Lucy paused, and craned her neck. "What is it dear? Have I upset you? What do you want me to say? You look so pale. Is there something else there?"

Muriel held herself tight and clasped her hands to stop herself from shaking. "Of course, there's something else there," she said with hardly a breath. "Can't you see it?"

Lucy peered through the glass, squinting with half an eye. "What else can there be?"

"In its place. What's in its place?"

"What can you mean? There's a space, a clearing. There's nothing, except… sky and shade." She looked up, her face filled with alarm. "What on earth has happened, dear? Tell me. Are you ill?" She stood up, and touched Muriel's feverish brow. "You are ill. You're burning up."

Muriel shook the fragile hand away.

"Of course I'm not ill. You're the frail one, dear Lucy. That's why we have to do this. Get your bag and coat. We must leave."

"I don't know what's got into you, Muriel dear. You've always been a little bit cockatoo, and I fear it's made you somewhat cockeyed with one eye roaming in some storm and the other dizzy in your head." She sat back down on her chair, shaking her head. "I have nothing but the roof over my head, and I'm not giving it up for a strange notion that's doing contortions in your head."

A lump entered Muriel's throat and lodged itself there as silence fell between them and her thoughts drifted to what lay ahead. No-one ever went up there. Not with the wind and its incessant wailing and the rain that soaked through clothes like paper. But she couldn't just sit there perched like an old bird, waiting to fall off. And the feeling that she would fall off was so strong now, she couldn't stop the impatient pounding that was knocking in her chest. And the rain, such dark, dreary rain. Black rain, she called it, because no-one had seen the sun for months. Surely, it was clearing now, for she could see the house in all its grit and grime. Yes, it was time. She was never so certain.

She stared at Lucy's face, poor simple, gentle Lucy, as innocent as a lamb in a butcher's yard, and the lump in her throat fractured like a splintering rock and tore up inside her. If only her breath didn't feel so heavy and her fear seem so real. She stood up, tall and thin, her cotton dress clinging to her thin bones. She couldn't escape the thought of what she had to do.

She scurried over to the table in the middle of the room, gathering tins and jars, shoving them into a cloth bag, then hurried out of the pantry into a side room where Lucy's bed was, dodging leaks from the gaping holes in the roof and throwing blankets and shawls into a bag. Provisions, that's what they needed. Bread, cheese. Not much else. Just enough until it was over. And it wasn't going to take long. She had to make sure it wouldn't take long. For Lucy's sake. What else could she do? Lucy wouldn't survive on her own.

Lucy looked up from the closed book on her lap, her face pleading like a helpless little girl. "At least tell me what's happened."

"There's no time. Put these on," she thrust the boots in Lucy's hand. "Hurry, before it's too late."

*****

"Mother always said you were as pig-headed as a pair of prim pyjamas," said Lucy, pulling on her boots.

"She always talked such nonsense," Muriel said, grabbing their bags, and as the words came out, an involuntary smile broke across her face at a memory when everything seemed normal, even when it never was. How could it have been? There was always the house peering at her from afar. The smile fell from her face as quickly as the drops of rain that were calling her.

They stepped out onto the hard stone ground, boots on their feet and a small bag each. The sting of the cold air made Muriel wince as the relentless rain drove into their faces and seeped through their thin coats. And yet, it wasn't the rain they needed protection from.

"Alright, you got me out, Muriel dear. Now tell me what's happened."

"Lucy dear, I'm going to die."

"What do you mean? Be more specific. Am I going to kill you?"

"I saw the house that no-one's built. I was lying beside the tree. It's come for me."

Lucy was silent. Her eyes were low but Muriel knew the sorrow her words brought to them.

"Don't speak like that. You know the house is not real."

Muriel looked at the stark, empty streets. How could Lucy not see what the house had done? A whole village plucked out of existence. The vacant dwellings that were like a row of graves. She turned into the alley that led up to the hill and eyed her surroundings with sadness. How still and dirty with grime the houses seemed despite the rain. As if sprinkled with death.

"Muriel dear, people leave," Lucy was saying. "It doesn't mean anything."

"They haven't just left, Lucy dear, they've vanished. Remember old Mr. Couldon, and little Suzie, and Felix the farmer's boy and all the others. No trace of them. How do you explain it, if it's not the house?"

"I think you've finally flipped the pancake on your head, dear, dear, Muriel... so what are you saying? It's now come for you? Are we taking a jolly excursion to your grave, Muriel dear? That's twisted, even for you, dear..." Muriel was silent. Lucy never did understand about the house. "...If Mother could see you now, out she'd pop, doing flip-flops and somersaults."

Muriel paused, panting at the steep incline and looked ahead. The top of the house was visible now. She held Lucy's hand, who was struggling, and pulled her up.

"Lucy dear, I'm not leaving you behind. If I go, you go."

Lucy stopped and took a deep breath. "That's very thoughtful of you, Muriel dear. Crazy and terrifying but quite thoughtful, nevertheless. If it's all the same to you, I'll stop here. My passing is an adventure I would rather not venture on just at the moment. Visit your gruesome house, if you must. And if it takes you, so be it, I shall miss you. But I rather have a book in my hand then die out here, befuddled and alone. The mind boggles what you had in mind, Muriel dear. Were you planning on wringing my neck like a chicken? I am no chicken, so let's not try and get me into the oven before my goose is cooked."

"Lucy dear, how will you get along? You've always been so, how can I put it, flippy."

"Flippy? What does that even mean?"

"Soppy, then."

"What can you mean? Emotional?"

"Positively dripping with it."

"And you were hoping to dry me out in the rain?"

"Dear Lucy, I was hoping we'd go together. I wouldn't worry about you if we were both dead."

"Dear, dear Muriel. You'd be dead and senseless. Not as senseless as you are now, but close enough. Your poor deteriorating body will not have a guilty bone to worry it."

"Yes, Lucy dear, but open your eyes. Can't you see it? Can't you hear it, calling? The last thing I want, Lucy dear, is for me to go to the house that no-one built, and leave you alone in the house, below."

A grey cloud formed over Muriel's head as the worry of her words hung over her. She could feel the windows of the house peering into her soul. She was halfway to death's door already. She shivered and stretched out her arm, reaching for Lucy's hand. But Lucy had turned away and was tottering back down the hill like a stubborn mule. How could she not hear the whispers melting in the rain?

> Your time has come little flower,
>
> your days are done,
>
> come cower beside the house you built,
>
> my little petal, my little fruit.

"Dear, dear Muriel," Lucy was shaking her head, mumbling to herself, as she carefully tackled the hill. "What you think I'll see in this house, I'll never know. Your dead corpse body?"

"At least, look at the house before dismissing my death as a flighty thing of fancy, Lucy dear. Don't make me come back for you afterwards."

Lucy half-turned and called back over her shoulder. "I will not go all the way up only to find that we are just a pair of silly women waiting for the house that no-one has built to kill us both."

"It's only a little further, Lucy dear, and if the house does not kill us we'll come back and have a cup of tea."

"Alright, Muriel dear. You've talked me into it. Only because I don't want you to be on that dreadful hill all alone. But I can tell you this, if we survive the house and this piddling rain, you won't hear the end of it."

*****

As they struggled up the hill, hand in hand like a pair of schoolgirls huddling for strength, Muriel felt the storm grip her with its power, trying to carry her away. She battled it, her shawl flying behind her, squeezing her throat, her dress like a wet flannel wrapping around her legs as she inched forward. She had the will of an ox inside the body of a feeble goat and so she pulled poor, reluctant Lucy up the last few steps and stopped to look at the majesty of destitution that loomed in front of them.

"Now do you see it?"

"I see nothing. Has it sunk? What carpet dust have you been swallowing, Muriel dear? Sometimes I wish I could see what you have in your head. You brought me up here for a strange notion and all I see is a dead tree and a fresh hole."

"Look closely, Lucy dear. Look into the hole."

"I will not. If I fall in, I won't be able to get out, again."

"Then don't fall in."

"I don't want some gaping hole to swallow me up, Muriel dear."

"Lucy dear. The house does not lie. It'll take us both. You'll see."

"Muriel, Muriel, if only you could hear yourself. The house no-one has built is talking to you. What a pity it is to have a derelict thing inside your derelict head."

"Stop fussing, Lucy dear. Lean on me, just hold onto me. What do you see?"

"A great big hole… and a beautiful hole it is… a revelation…"

Muriel had stopped listening. The arched, grimy doors before her opened invitingly and she stepped in, pulling Lucy in after her. She wallowed in the magnificence of the decaying beauty, the high ceiling; the grimy broken windows twisted with foliage that had forced their way in and were now creeping and winding their way down the crumbling walls. Such a fragile thing it was, threatening to fall with one breath. One breath and it would all be over. The tiled floor, sweeping with colours, dazzled her as she grabbed Lucy's hand and they slipped in like ice dancers tumbling and sliding in an icy grave. And in that instance, as they slid over the floor of the house that no-one built, she heard a crunch, an icy, pure, decisive crunch, as all around her darkened.

"You Pickle-brained funnel, you've broken my bones..." yelped a pitiful creature groaning on the ground.

Muriel turned to look, but the crumpled creature on the ground was hazy, as if a cloud had come between them. Her voice, distant as the night, dissipated into the corners of the hall. She slumped down beside the creature, taking in the derelict, gaping hall that would soon consume them and waited for the end as if the time was stamped there for all to see. But something was not right. As the walls around her crumbled with tears of dust, and the house spewed and vomited debris through its sockets, a terrible vision appeared in Muriel's eyes. She saw the house, a degraded monument, worn away by years of neglect, beckoning, not her, but poor, sick Lucy. There was no crisp, precise, unswerving death here. There was something worse. Her eyes shot in the direction of the windows, the broken soul of the house rejecting her, leaving her behind. And as the walls fell in a deafening storm of stone and mortar and the ground cracked open, the house sang its song of sighs, melting in a melody of whispers, and she heard the tuneful retort of the house in her ear:

> Pity the one not belonging
>
> The house you built is done with calling
>
> Do not bring
>
> A stranger in
>
> The house will not sing for the quick and the living

Muriel covered her ears. The house did not want her and she was alone. It was calling, but not for her. She looked at Lucy, ashamed of what she had done. The poor innocent lay there, her eyes black with pain, her voice stifled by the whispering melodies that drifted in the air. Muriel shut her eyes, consumed by the vision she had seen before. And like all the visions of the villagers before, she could not hold onto it. There was Lucy, diminishing, vanishing, reeling like a speck of dirt in the pupils of her eyes. And as she lost all who entered the house through her eyes, into the night, so too was she losing Lucy. She sat where they once sat, a shrivelling heap diminishing into nothing as the house called her in:

> Come, come my little one
>
> come in and let us be done
>
> scatter the floor with your broken bones
>
> in the house she built for you alone

The stairs, unhinged, swung precariously over Muriel's head as destruction rained around her. She cradled Lucy's soft, bony body as it disintegrated in her arms and disappeared amidst the falling pillars. The dust spilt through her fingers and she grew frantic, sweeping the rubble in search of Lucy. The air crammed like ash into her throat and an opening, where the walls had collapsed, appeared. Through it, she saw an old oak tree lying dormant on the ground and a few feet away a figure, lifeless and pale amidst the storm's melodious tones. Her features were crisp and pure in the dirt, her eyes open but unseeing. She crawled towards it, her hands black and torn in the dirt. And as the walls came raining down, slow, dusty rain hanging in the air like an expectation, Muriel swept up the body in a bundle of arms and legs. She cradled the lifeless figure, her tears staining her crusty face, and under the black rain that painted the sky, she couldn't help but call out her final reproach.

"Now do you believe me, Lucy dear? Now do you see it?"

She heard nothing back for the house was broken, falling away into a dusty storm. The house that Muriel built.

Beautiful Words, Where Are You?
By Deborah Collins

I have no words:
they've flown like birds
flipped out of sight
evading moonlight
that makes a trail
like a giant snail
glowing
flowing

I have few words:
they form small herds
or little flocks
like scattered socks
I chase them
replace them
fluttering
puttering

I have some words:
their lines are blurred
they're coming back
sprouting through cracks
I plant them in pots
in sheltered spots

showing

growing

My words are steady

but still not ready

I water them

try not to slaughter them

warm them

reform them

refining

defining

shining...

ignoring all maligning

popping, not stopping

close to cropping

in my garden

where frosts no longer harden

undeterred

beautiful words

Even a Monkey Can Fall from a Tree
by Drew Payne

Day One

Nick stretched out in bed. Had he really behaved like that? Wasn't that how gays behaved in the bad old seventies? Not that he knew, being born in 1996. Why had he been so silly? Anything could have happened to him there, and he would have been responsible for it. But he'd done so much all at once, touched and been touched by so many men, and it had felt good then. Now… Had he really let himself go so far?

He moved under the sheets, trying to find a cool spot in the bedclothes. His body was still tired even after all that sleep.

The Platinum Jubilee Bank Holiday gave him a four-day long weekend. Looking towards it he didn't know what he would do with himself. Everyone he knew seemed to be planning something for it, filling up their time with events and Nick was looking on from the side-lines again. It was the prospect of spending the long weekend alone in his small studio flat, getting on top of himself, that he was dreading most.

He'd seen the advert, online, four days ago. The picture of the two naked men caught his attention, as he read the advert an excitement came over him, but tinged with guilt. The advert was for a gay sex party, on the Bank Holiday Friday, at a Vauxhall gay club. He'd never been to a sex club. He always saw himself as one of those good gays, the ones who met their boyfriends, settled down together, got married, and adopted a child or dog together. He hadn't managed it though, never had a boyfriend for any length of time, and now he was single again. Why shouldn't he go to a sex party? Why shouldn't he live a little on the wild side? He'd been so good for too long. He saved a copy of the advert onto his laptop.

Again, he stretched out in bed. His body felt so tired and stiff, his shoulders and lower back had a dull ache. He needed a shower, to wash away last nights "sins", to clean his skin at least. He turned over onto his side, and the ache continued in his lower back. There was now a tingling sensation to his lips, no around his lips, under the skin of his cheeks. What was wrong with him?

He felt excited and more than a bit dirty last night. He arrived at the club and paid the entrance fee. Inside he found men having sex together in so many different parts of the club, and he had sex there too. He kissed men he didn't know and had sex with men he didn't know, sex he'd never imagined he'd have with strangers.

He left the club in the early hours of the morning, his body felt slick with sweat and stained with… well he knew what. In his Uber home, the uncomfortable feelings started, had he really done that?

His full bladder pushed him into movement. He sat up in bed and it hit him. He was exhausted, his body ached with it. It was as if he'd not slept a moment last night. And with sitting upright, a heavy and blunt pain hit the front of his head. He closed his eyes against it. Had he caught the flu? In June?

Day Two

Nick looked at his face in the bathroom mirror. There was a rash around his mouth. He hadn't imagined it. There were seven spots along his lower lip. They were small, round spots that seemed white in colour. He gently pressed his finger against one of them. It wasn't painful but the spot felt hard, fluid filled. Underneath it was that tingling sensation, which was getting worse. What was happening to him?

He'd been ill all yesterday, his body aching with the flu, and this morning nothing had changed, no his symptoms were getting worse. He woke up with a fever, his body sweaty with it. He was so tired. What was wrong with him?

He left the bathroom, returning to his flat's main room, and collapsed back onto his bed. He needed to rest, again.

Day Five

Lying sideways on his sofa was comfortable, as near to comfortable as he could find. The rash on his face was worse, his jaw was covered in eight, large spots which had turned into angry and fluid filled blisters. The rash was appearing on his buttocks now, small and solid spots. The pain from it was stopping him from sleeping and paracetamol didn't seem to touch it. With the flu on top of it, it was miserable. Daytime television was so disappointing, but he left it on so that its noise washed over him.

His phone's ringtone made him start; God was this work? He picked it up and saw it was his friend Garth. He answered it and Garth's face filled the screen. Garth's dark hair was casually ruffled but his dark beard was still neatly clipped short.

"Hi," he told Garth.

"Work's shit so I'm skiving off for five minutes. You all right?"

"I'm off work, I've got the flu."

"But your face. That rash is nasty."

"I'm having a reaction to something."

"It looks like Monkey Pox."

"What?"

"I've seen pictures online and your rash looks really like it."

"Shit no," Nick said, his left hand touching his face.

*****

Nick hung up his phone. He'd managed to get through to his GP on the third attempt. He only spoke to a receptionist, a sharply efficient voiced woman. She took a list of his symptoms and then told him a *"clinician"* would call him back within forty-eight hours.

He lay back on the sofa, careful not to lay on his buttocks, all he could do was wait.

Day Six

He paused at the bottom of the stairs. Walking down the two flights to his building's front door left him tired out. He was only twenty-six, he couldn't be this tired? He took a deep breath and opened the building's front door.

On the other side was a middle-aged man, dressed in an oversized high-vis jacket, with three crates of shopping stacked at his feet.

It was Nick's first online grocery shop and it had been surprisingly easy.

"Busy day today," the man said.

"Yes, it must be," Nick agreed, before he bent down and lifted the bags of shopping out of the top crate.

It only took a moment to empty his shopping out of those crates.

As he retrieved the last bag, the man said, "That's a nasty rash on your face. You need to get it seen to."

"Thanks, I'm waiting to hear back from my doctor."

It was after he'd closed the front door, after he'd seen the man taking away the empty crates, that realisation struck him. He shouldn't have opened the door without a mask. That delivery man saw his rash. What if the man reported back to his office? What if they refused to deliver to him because he was an infection risk? He was so stupid. He touched his face, the rash rough and obvious under his fingers.

He must get his shopping back up to his flat. He was tired already. He started to thread the bags onto both of his hands.

Day Seven

At least his fever had stopped now. It was a little after one o'clock and his clothes weren't damp with sweat. It was one relief. The rash on his face was still angry and the pain from it was only getting worse. And the rash on his buttocks was equally as painful.

Again he was lying face down on his bed, it was one of the few positions that was comfortable.

His phone rang, pulling his attention towards it. He kept it close to him now. He was ill and on his own, having it with him was comforting. He answered it and found it was a video call from a "Private Number".

A woman's face filled his screen. Her short, brown hair framing her face.

"Is that Nicholas Todd?" The woman asked him.

"Yes," he replied.

"I'm Dr Stratford-Hill. You rang the surgery because you haven't been well. What's been happening?"

"I've had the flu since Saturday."

"The flu?"

"I've had a temperature, my joints ache and I'm so tired."

"And that rash on your face?"

"It started on Saturday too. Little spots but it got worse and... Well, its on my buttocks too. A friend video called me the other day and he said it looks like Monkey Pox."

"It certainly does. This is a tricky question but have you had sex with other men, before the rash came out?"

"Yes, I..." He couldn't tell her about going to a sex club. She was a doctor but that was going too far. "Yes, I have."

"It certainly seems like Monkey Pox." Hearing her words say it wasn't reassuring. It was a sinking realisation, and it was his fault. His mistake had left him infected. "You need to stay indoors and away from other people until your rash fully heals up. I'll prescribe you some naproxen."

"Is that to treat it?"

"No, it's a painkiller. Hopefully it'll help you get some sleep. Monkey Pox is a virus. Your body will fight it off but it can take a few weeks to do that. I'll give you a fit note for a month but you can go back to work before then, but only when your rash has fully healed."

"A fit note?" he asked.

"We used to call them sick certificates."

"Do I have to collect it from the surgery?"

"No, I'll email it to you. Now take care of yourself, eat well and rest. Call the surgery back if you get worse or have any concerns."

"I will."

Then the call was over.

He watched his blank phone for a long moment.

*****

The ping from his phone made him open his eyes. He'd slipped into a doze and it felt good, just casually sleeping. He pushed himself up on his sofa and the pain from the rash on his face pushed away the last of the warm sleep. He winced at the pain in his buttocks too. He hated this, he was so pathetic, this pain was ruling him. He unlocked his phone.

The ping had been the email from his GP, with his Fit note attached. With a few taps of his finger, he forwarded it to Hector, his manager at work. He didn't need to open the Fit note, let Hector sort that out. It was Hector's job.

Nick leant back on his sofa, trying to find some position that was comfortable.

Day Eight

He was still in bed and it was coming up to mid-day, but why get up? The pain from his rash was always there. It woke him again and again overnight. At least staying in bed he could get comfortable. If he got up, he'd have to dress and clothes made his rash worse. He stretched out in bed, the itch on his face was still there too. He hadn't shaved since the rash started, he couldn't risk damaging it, and now the stubble was itching like crazy.

His phone pinged. He pulled himself up in bed and reached for it. An email. Someone was thinking of him. He missed people, stupidly but he did. Garth always went on at him that he needed to be more gregarious, but... It wasn't that easy. But he missed people, just being around them. It was stupid.

The email was from Hector, simply acknowledging Nick's email, but nothing more. His Fit note was still attached to the reply, typical of Hector. Nick opened it, what had the GP said about him, and the first he saw was his diagnosis, Monkey Pox. It said Monkey Pox. Hector read he had Monkey Pox. Shit, he'd been so stupid.

He was stupid, stupid. If he hadn't gone to that sex club... He wouldn't have Monkey Pox. He'd done all this to himself.

Day Nine

Nick closed his laptop. Why had he gone down that rabbit hole?

He'd done a Google search on Monkey Pox, it was to educate himself. It was a virus but he knew little more.

On the NHS website, he read how he caught it, coming in contact with someone else who had it, but little more. Not why he'd caught it.

His search almost drowned him in results, there was so much out there, so many people had their own opinions. He started reading by clicking on whichever links spoke to him, the ones that offered him more information, but quickly an overriding theme jumped out at him. So many of them shouted out that gay men who caught Monkey Pox caught it at their own risk. They shouted out that gay men were immoral, perverse and dirty, that they sought out this infection. Many said gay men "deserved" Monkey Pox, punishment for their sexual behaviour. Others shouted out that gay men didn't "deserve" the vaccination. Reading those websites caught at the back of his throat, but he carried on. One led to another, his mouse pulling him to the next piece of judgement, and all of them screaming at him it was his fault.

Twitter was worse, but it was so easy to read them and his eye followed them down the screen. Tweets angrily proclaiming judgement and condemnation on gay men with Monkey Pox. Voices shouting for chastity, celibacy and modesty; shouts for legs to be kept together and hands to be kept to themselves.

He'd done this all to himself. Willingly he'd gone to that sex club. No one forced him to go there. He'd enjoyed the anonymous sex there. Now he was paying the price for it. It was his fault.

He stroked his hand over the lid of his closed laptop. He didn't hate being gay but he wasn't happy with it. He wanted a boyfriend; he hated always being on his own. If he had a boyfriend then his life would be so much better. He could join so much more of society as a married couple, be one of those acceptable gays, entertain friends as a couple and not just be judged by his
sex life. He could finally come out to his parents because he'd have a boyfriend by his side.

The rash on his face was aching again.

Day Twelve

It was nearly a fortnight now, fourteen days kept in his own home. The rash on his face was still angry, fluid filled blisters, pushing their way through the stubble on his face. He still couldn't risk seeing anyone in person. But he was so alone.

He hadn't had a great social life but he wanted it all back now, even the things he did on his own. He wanted to meet Garth for a coffee after work, to gossip with Garth, to go to a gay bar and listen to Garth bitch about the other men there. He wanted to go to the cinema, television wasn't the same. He'd go straight after work, when the cinemas were half empty, and he'd get lost in a film on his own. Shit, he missed travelling on the Underground, watching all the other people in the same carriage.

He even missed work. What a thing to admit. He must be crazy. But he wanted to be back there. His job wasn't great. Most of his time was spent assessing people for mortgages, or assessing their risk of not repaying them, and most of those people failed the criteria. When he'd studied Maths and Financial Planning, at university, he'd imagined himself making important financial choices at, but... It was a job and at least he enjoyed working with numbers. He could always rely on numbers.

Most of his work colleagues were so straight and conservative, with a small and a capital C, their lives so different from his. He kept quiet at work, don't rock the boat, don't make a target of himself, don't be gay. He'd hear enough homophobic jokes in the office's banter, so he was careful, so careful he was still in the closet.

It was so stupid but he missed all that. It hadn't been this bad in lockdown, but he hadn't been so alone then. He'd had all those team meetings on Zoom, and he had remote work to fill his time. Now all he had was Facetime with Garth, and that wasn't the same.

The work WhatsApp group. He still had that. It was mostly people gossiping about work, bitching about clients, boasting about their achievements. He could at least be, sort of, close to work with it.

Nick reached for his phone and opened WhatsApp on it. His work group was halfway down the screen but when he opened it all he got was a message that he was locked out of it Shit, something was wrong. Someone had shared client details or something. It had happened before.

He closed his phone.

Day Fourteen

Nick relaxed. He could sit comfortably on the sofa now. It was mid-morning and his painkillers were still working. He'd been able to shower, and even do some yoga exercises afterwards. He could still feel the tingle around his mouth but the pain had eased. Finally, could he be getting better? Simply sitting comfortably was a win.

The buzz from his flat's intercom made him start. Who was it?

When he answered it, his sister's voice boomed out.

"Nick! Open up! It's me, Lottie!"

Almost on reflex, he buzzed her into the building.

What did Lottie want? She usually rang him and arranged their meetings. How did she know he was at home? He couldn't let her get too close to him, his rash hadn't dried up so he was still infectious.

He opened his front door and retreated back into his flat, he needed to keep a distance from her.

In jeans and a silk blouse, her dyed blonde hair in a ponytail, Lottie strode into his flat, the words pouring out of her mouth.

"Flick and I planned a girly day out in London. then she bails on me, at the last minute. Fucking typical. So I thought I'd drop in on my baby brother. Mum said you've got the flu, so I thought I'd cheer... What the fuck is on your face?"

Lottie stopped a few feet in front of him, distaste filling her face.

Nick clamped his hand over his mouth but it was too late.

"Nick? Your face?"

"I've... I've got Monkey Pox."

"That's disgusting! You get that from screwing around. I thought better of you."

"It's not my fault."

"Oh God! I could catch it from you!"

"Not like that."

"You selfish bastard! I've got children and I could catch it. You're so thoughtless!"

"Lottie..." He tried to protest but she was already rushing out of his flat, still shouting at him.

The flat's door slammed shut and the room returned to silence.

"Fuck," he dropped down onto his sofa. "Fuck..."

He'd upset her, he shouldn't have done that, he should have... But what? He'd upset her and Lottie never remained silent.

Day Seventeen

Nick changed the channel again. There was nothing on worth watching, nothing two steps above mindless. He'd watched too much television and was tired of it. Why couldn't something just be interesting? Was it him? A week ago, he'd subscribed to streaming TV. Before he said he never would.

He used to go out, he'd meet Garth and they'd talk and talk. He used to go to the cinema. He never had time for television, now it was all he had to fill his time.

His phone rang. A distraction? He snatched it up. It was Miranda from work, gossip queen Miranda. Why was she calling him?

He answered it, "Hello?"

"Hi Nicholas," Miranda's too bright voice said. "How are you?"

"All right. Getting better." He wasn't going to tell her the truth.

"That Monkey Pox must be awful. I've a cousin who was a nurse and…"

"How… How do you know I've got it?" He asked, interrupting her.

"It's so terrible but Hector told people. He said your GP told him. It's just typical of him, he was always a half-arsed manager."

"He told people?"

"It went around the office like diarrhoea. Oh, sorry but you know what I mean."

"Yes," he mumbled.

"It was terrible what people were saying. Lenny was being such a prick about it, well about you."

"Lenny?" He usually avoided the man, Lenny being one of the office's self-appointed alpha males.

"He's been making really bad jokes. Well, he called them jokes but they weren't that funny."

"He's been joking about me?"

"They were stupid things. Like, how do you know a monkey's gay? It's got the pox. How do you stop yourself getting Monkey Pox? Be straight. See, they aren't that good."

"They're nasty." He could hear all that homophobia about Monkey Pox, he'd read online, echoing again.

"He posted them all over the work WhatsApp group."

"Is that why it was closed down?"

"It isn't closed down," she said.

"But I can't access it."

"Hector probably locked you out of it. He was worried you'd see it. You know Hector."

"Locked me out?"

"Yes, typical Hector. Now I've got to go. Suzi's back from her break and you know how she is. Ciao."

"Er..." But the phone went silent in his ear. She was gone.

*****

Hector didn't answer his phone on Nick's third attempt. Anger pushed up into Nick's throat, voicemail again! Hector was avoiding him. The man was avoiding him, how could he?

Then the idea snapped into his head. He'd ring Hector's landline. The man couldn't screen that. On the second ring Hector answered it.

"Hector Jones, Financial Assessment."

"It's Nicolas. I want a word."

"Look, this has to be quick. I'm very busy."

"You told everyone I've got Monkey Pox! I didn't say you could. That's breaking confidentiality."

"I didn't do that," Hector's voice snapped back.

"Everyone in the office knows I've got it and I only told you."

"I didn't tell everyone."

"Then how does everyone know?"

"I only told a few people. It's not my fault they told everyone else."

"I didn't say you could tell anyone."

"But technically you didn't say not to tell anyone," Hector said.

"It was a medical diagnosis. You don't tell other people that!"

"And you've made enough mistakes at work that I've had to cover up."

"This isn't the … I haven't made mistakes at work."

"Well other people have."

"And you locked me out of the WhatsApp group."

"It was only banter but people like you get offended at the slightest of things."

"People like who?"

"I've got to go, I've got a very important meeting and we're only going around in circles."

"What?" But he only received silence in reply, Hector had hung up on him.

Nick stared at his phone. Should he call HR? But they were as useless as Hector. Was there any point? He'd been right to stay in the closet, at work, but that was all gone now. Was he now Nicholas, the office queer? Shit, shit, shit…

He replaced his phone on the sofa, next to him.

Day Nineteen

Nick lay on his sofa, the television playing unwatched. It was gone six o'clock and he should be getting himself some dinner, but he wasn't hungry. Food bored him. It had been boring him for days.

The intercom's buzzing made him jump. Who was this? No one had visited him in ages.

He pulled himself up from his sofa and answered the intercom.

"Hello?"

"It's me, let me in," Garth's voice barked out at him.

He buzzed Garth into the building.

Only a few moments later, Garth was bounding into his flat. Garth was dressed in his work clothes, chinos and an ironed cotton shirt, his dark hair was ruffled, and he was full of his endless energy.

"God, you look like shit!" Garth exclaimed.

"I'm better, I am," Nick replied.

"It's really got to you, being on your own, I didn't realise."

"I'm sorry… I…"

"Come here, mate," Garth opened out his arms and took a step towards him.

"No! You can't! I'm still infectious!" He backed away; he couldn't infect his best friend.

"And I've been vaccinated," Garth replied, pulling Nick into a hug.

For a long and quiet moment, he just gave himself over to the hug. Garth's body was so solid, so re-assuring and his arms held Nick closely. He could smell Garth's deodorant, and the fabric conditioner on his shirt. Nick could feel the movement of Garth's chest as he slowly breathed. It was so long since someone had hugged him, since anyone had touched him. He blinked back the tears, it was stupid to cry, but he couldn't stop the tears and then he was crying like some baby.

"Let it out," Garth said. "God, it must have been shit."

Garth's arms squeezed him that bit closer.

*****

He bit into another slice of pizza. It was hot and greasy and tasted of too much cheese, and it was so good.

The two of them sat on his sofa, with the greasy pizza box between them. It had been Garth's idea to order a pizza and some beers, and he was so glad Garth did. Eating with someone else was so much easier.

"And your manager told them all?" Garth said, continuing their conversation.

"He told people I've got Monkey Pox and now I've been outed at work."

"Fuck," Garth bit into his slice of pizza.

"And I've been locked out of the work WhatsApp group because it's full of homophobic jokes."

"Fuck, fuck."

"How was the vaccine?" Nick asked, between mouthfuls of pizza.

"Not bad, the worst part was waiting for it. I had to queue-up for two hours that Saturday morning, outside a Sexual Health clinic in South London."

"What did you do?"

"Fired-up Grindr on my phone and did some cruising. I got two dates out of it."

"I wish I could do that."

"You can," Garth said. "Just log onto Grindr."

"I went to a sex club on the Jubilee Bank Holiday."

"Good for you. You need to get laid."

"It's where I caught Monkey Pox."

"Fuck, sorry. But don't let that put you off. Enjoy yourself, it's not a sin."

"I suppose."

"Did you enjoy yourself?" Garth asked.

"Well... Yes, I did," Nick admitted. Monkey Pox had coloured his memory of it, but he had enjoyed it. A guilty pleasure?

"There's nothing wrong with that."

He took another bite of pizza and chewed it slowly.

"I don't want to go back to work," he admitted.

"Yeah, I see."

"I can't face seeing Hector, my manager."

"Fuck him, he's a twat."

"Could I take them to an Industrial Tribunal?" The idea suddenly jumped into his mind, it would make Hector squirm.

"Have you got a spare five grand?"

"No?"

"It's what I tell people when they ring work asking that. Its fucking expensive and you've got to have a shit load of evidence."

"Shit." For a moment the idea was nice.

"Put in a HR complaint, I'll help you write it. That will fuck up your manager, even just with the paperwork."

"And I could vote with my feet. Get a new job."

"Yeah. You've got a good degree and they're always crying out for people in finance."

"Yes, and it would make a lot more work for Hector."

"Good, fuck the twat."

"Hell no. He's so ugly and boring."

Garth let out a roar of laughter. Nick had so missed this, just being with Garth, with his friend.

He took another bite of his pizza slice.

Day Twenty-One

Even with the shower turned off, his tiny bathroom was still full of steam. His own, little sauna. He didn't open the bathroom door, he just enjoyed the hot steam, for a moment, as he dried his body.

Once dry, he pushed the bathroom's door open and let the hot steam flow out. He took his towel and wiped off the steam from the bathroom mirror. He could check the progress of his beard.

His face stared back at him but it was different. His strawberry blond beard was still short but there were only two spots left on his face, and they were dried scabs now. The other spots had gone, in their place was smooth and shiny pink new skin. He touched one of those new patches of skin. It was flat and soft under his finger.

The spots were gone. It was all over. Monkey Pox had gone and he was clear of it.

He ran his hand over his lower face, his fingers searching out those new patches of skin. It was over, finished. He was free from it.

His eyes filled up with tears.

Day Twenty-Seven

Nick sat at his desk and stared at his computer screen. It was only mid-morning but already he couldn't be bothered with his work. He used to pride himself on the quality of his work but what was the point? They didn't value him here, he could see that.

He only came back to work yesterday.

When he'd entered the office, yesterday morning, before he even got to his desk, Hector called him into his office. As soon as the door was closed, Hector said;

"People have expressed some concerns about you coming back. I need you to not use the staff toilet on this floor, you can use the public toilet in reception, and not to use the staff room"

"No," Nick replied. He hadn't even sat at his desk and Hector was dumping on him.

"I'm not being unreasonable because people have asked, and it's no more than we did with Covid."

"This is not the same!" His anger was pushing up into his chest. "That was a pandemic and we worked from home. I had a skin infection but I'm not infectious now."

"How can we be certain of that?"

He bit down on his anger, not swearing in Hector's face.

"Because I was only infectious when I had the rash and that's all healed up now," he pointed to his chin to emphasis it, though he had kept his short beard to hide the shiny patches of new skin on his face. "I was off work the whole time I was infectious. I saw no one and it was hell."

"People are still worried, especially after Covid. I'm thinking about hygiene in the office."

"You were quick to tell everyone when I had Monkey Pox. Well you can now tell them all that I'm not infectious!"

"Nicholas, you're not being helpful. I need to think of the welfare of everyone in the office."

"Then you sort it out, I'm going to do my work."

He left there before he had to listen to any more of Hector's whining. Garth had warned him this could happen, and again Garth was right.

It didn't take long to see that Hector hadn't told people he wasn't infectious. Quickly he saw that people around the office were avoiding him. Rebekah, who he used to share his cubicle with, had moved to a desk on the far side of the office. If he left his desk, he found people were avoiding him. They stepped out of his way, leaving a large space between them, some even looked away with an embarrassed expression. Miranda certainly looked embarrassed, when he walked past her at the photocopier. She didn't stop by his desk, trying to get some gossip out of him, as she had so often done.

Also, repeatedly he overheard Lenny telling loud and unfunny homophobic jokes to his alpha male mates, around the office, as if the man didn't have any work to do, as if he wanted Nick to overhear him.

Was he being paranoid, did they so openly not want him here?

Mid-day, as he left the staff toilet, he found himself confronted by Lenny.

"Hey, you were told not to use that," Lenny protested.

"Fuck off!" Nick snapped back.

"I'm reporting this to Hector! You're a public health risk!"

"So fucking sue me," Nick hissed and walked away.

For a moment it felt good, he'd never liked Lenny. But when he sat down at his desk, he couldn't avoid it, was this how he was seen now, a public health risk?

He left work yesterday on the stroke of five o'clock. He didn't offer to "help out" others who could barely do their own work or help sort out the mess someone else made. He wasn't staying late. As he walked past Hector's open office door, he sped up. He didn't want Hector calling out to him, asking him to sort out someone else's problem. He was meeting Garth after work, and his friend was more important.

Now he had three open assessments on his computer, all of them were too big a risk to offer mortgages to. He needed to contact them with the bad news, but… It could wait. He was going to look after himself, for once. He clicked on the first link, opening a recruitment website. He would start here.

As he started his search, his phone pinged. He glanced at it and saw it was a text from Garth.

"How are you doing?" Garth's text read.

"Looking for a new job." He texted back.

A moment later he received three thumbs-up emojis from Garth.

Day Ninety-Seven

The chair was uncomfortable, but weren't they always at interviews?

Nick looked at the three-person panel in front of him, two women and a man, but the middle-aged woman sat in the middle, Mrs Ford, was the one in charge. When he entered this interview and saw that, it was reassuring.

"Mr Todd," Mrs Ford said, as she lent back in her chair, "I don't want to put you on the spot but I do want to ask you this. You're very qualified for this job but why do you want to come and work for this council. We can't offer you the bonuses and perks you're getting in your current job. Why do you want to leave the private sector?"

Because he was tired of working in such a stupid and toxic environment, that he had to leave his job before it brought him down again and his research had shown that this council really did value their LGBTQ staff. But he couldn't say that, not straight out at an interview.

"I want to do financial planning that is a benefit to people's lives, even in a small way. Where I work, most of my work is assessing people's risk for a mortgage, and most people I'm given fail the assessment. I have to inform them they're not getting a mortgage. It is soul destroying. I want to work somewhere where I can make a positive difference with my job."

"And you think you can do that at this council?" Carole Rahman, the other woman on the panel, asked.

"Yes. Even if it's just finding a way to stretch a budget to fund another thing. I have a way with numbers, I like working out how to use them," he said. Were his answers sounding too woolly now?

"I think we've heard enough to easily make our decision," Mrs Ford smiled broadly back at him.

Safe Space by Frances Ogiemwense

Walking to the station

Through the phlegm of the nation

Your early morning smoke

about to make me choke

And now my daily mask

Make it even more a task

My students say

"East Ham miss, that's rough!"

I say "It's OK I'm tough"

But as I overtake

It's too easy to overrate

The price of being cool

To put up with all these fools

The pressure of the stress

is just too much duress

As the straps of your backpack hit me in the face

I ain't sure that I'm winning

This 'ting called human race

Sometimes I feel

It's just a disgrace

But still I give love, each push and each shove

Trying to get nearer, trying to get clearer

To shine in God's good grace

To finally find home

To find my safe space.

In The Rose Garden by Dharma Paul

A brisk, constitutional walk has meant for me regular circuits broadly in range of where I live. I say brisk but by the standards of fellow pedestrians, it is a steady stride.

Within one such circuit, there is a fenced off section of the local park. Within that section, a wooden walkway and metal screens encircle a rose garden. There were no roses at this point of the year.

I had previously seen or thought I had seen the young man a number of times, sat there on one of the benches. He was either reading or staring at a book. Over an extended period of time, we had reached a stage of exchanging greetings.

After what seemed the exchange of a large number of greetings, I was confident it was him. In any case, one day I took what still strikes me as the adventurous step of asking if he did not mind a moment's company, meaning my sitting on the same bench as him a few minutes.

He said, "Yes, please do."

He said this with what I recognised as superficial adroitness. I thought I also detected, at the edge of things, a certain alertness. This was although he expressed no outward strength of feeling either way.

On closer examination, I estimated he was by then in his early twenties, experimenting with a beard and also trying on contact lenses. He was still at a point in his life when he did not at all consider himself lucky to have time to sit in the park, over a book.

I recognised the book as a slender Argentinian volume in translation.

I am unsure if he recognised me then or later, this, my twenty-something, younger self. Perhaps he could not. I have changed. These days I am stout. What little hair remains on my head is white.

Perhaps this made the idea of my sitting with him for a moment less of a source of alarm to him. It is a quiet place but remains part of what is in many ways a still harder, colder, and even more anonymous city than of old.

"What's the book like?" I asked, thinking at the time I knew the answer, though later I was not so sure.

"He's a good writer. It makes the time pass." He smiled, politely. "You know him?" He presented the cover of the book to me.

"I do. He made the time pass for me too once. He did it interestingly, I thought. I used to wonder how he did it so... concisely."

He looked momentarily interested. "Are you a writer?"

"No. I used to teach in schools. I have to do a lot of writing in my current job but not of that sort," I said, pointing to his volume with what I hoped was a deflecting gesture.

"What's your job?"

I was reluctant to go into detail; and replied with mock self-importance: "I'm what they call a frontline social care worker."

He seemed less interested but said in a way I thought politely intended, "That sounds like a busy job. Do you have time to read?"

"I have less time to read than I did. So I don't read so... promiscuously." I could tell he liked the way I put it and perhaps did not feel quite so ready for a disappointing encounter, this bookish but still unworldly, young person.

I momentarily thought I saw in him one who might seem to others as if he felt himself in some insufferable way *above* them.

"How do you relax?"

"I don't," I said; then with a degree more sincerity added, "I find knowing I've maybe done a good day's work and some of the day's chores relaxes me... a bit... That and walking, with some vigour." I made a gesture indicating, I hoped, such a degree of vigour.

"And that's good enough?" he asked, with a smile I found somewhere between pleasing, teasing and, I thought, just a little sceptical.

"Not always but much more so than I expected."

"You're lucky," he said, looking in to the distance as if at something faraway.

"I don't always feel it," I retorted, "but I keep on... keeping at it. That currently works for me. Sort of. For now."

I did not know what to make of his gesture in reply. His look felt a little too extended. These things made me uncomfortable and even momentarily put out. I got up, made my farewells and continued, with some relief, upon my circuit.

You'll have to make do with me by Frank Crocker

Tom Hardy couldn't make it
Henry Cavill has flown away
Bradley Cooper's held in traffic
Not much more that I can I say?

Idris Elba's sent a sick note
Justin Bieber's been excused
Roger Moore is pushing Daisies
David Beckham's just confused

Chris Hemsworth's got a yoga class
George Clooney's got the flu
Hugh Jackman's way down under
But he sends his love to you.

Ryan Reynolds at his soccer club
Somewhere in north Wales
Jason Statham's got a puncture
With all that, that entails.

Gerard Butler's pulled a muscle
On his latest action flick
A shame they couldn't *all* come
You would have had your pick.

Michael Bublé would have sung

Smooth, really nice,

Daniel Craig just text to say

He's stuck indoors with Rachel Weiss.

Time Grinds to a Halt in the Coffee Shop
by Sarah Winslow

I finish the medium-level Sudoku, toss my pen on the table, close my eyes momentarily as I think regretfully about the piece of lemon drizzle cake I couldn't justify paying two pounds for, take a sip of my latte and look up. Something is wrong.

It takes me more than a few seconds to process. Everything, everyone is slowing down. Where ten minutes earlier it was all bustling busyness when I collected my coffee from the counter, it now looks like a slow-motion film.

Even the steam from the machines is slowing down, hovering in the air. The girl at the till and the four or five customers appear to be moving through water. Getting slower. Grinding to a halt.

And then there is no movement whatsoever. Everything, everyone is imprisoned in time. The barista is frozen in the act of putting a plastic lid on a paper cup. Two customers who were in animate conversation a moment ago both have their mouths open and hands suspended in mid-air gestures.

I make sure I can move. Take a sip of coffee. Yes, I'm perfectly normal.

I look around. The pink-haired older lady is caught in the act of turning the page. The man in the woolly hat has his cup half-raised, the steam from his coffee frozen in mid-air. A small boy is about to explode a bag of crisps all over the table. A mum is on her way to the loo guiding a tiny frizzy-haired girl ahead of her; it looks like she's left her handbag on the back of the pushchair, and there's a suspicious looking man hovering nearby, eyeing the handbag.

I get up gently and weave my way amongst these statues. I wonder how long the spell will last. I gently take the bag of crisps from the boy's hand and open it carefully, move the mum's handbag, burying it under a blanket in the pushchair and finally help myself to a large piece of lemon drizzle cake.

On the way back to my table I pass a nice-looking blond man staring sadly at his phone; the message reads: alex, yr a luvly guy but ive met someone else. sorry M

Before devouring my cake I quickly take out a scrap of paper and scribble my younger sister's phone number and a short message, and place it next to Alex's coffee cup.

I'm halfway through my cake when there's a hissing from the coffee machine and very slowly life starts up again. The pink-haired woman turns her page. The small boy eats his crisps carefully, the would-be thief looks confused, then walks out the door. Alex sees the note I've left him and looks interested. I finish up the crumbs and start on the difficult-level Sudoku.

The Forgotten Tree by Shah Obaid

Once there stood a tree so grand,
In the park where people roamed,
Animals and birds found shelter under its shade,
And it became a place where memories were formed.

But one day, it was cut down to the ground,
Its branches and leaves were taken away,
People hardly noticed the lack of sound,
And the memory of the old tree began to fray.

But from its wood, a bench was made,
Fixed in the same park where it once stood,
Old folks now rest, tired and jaded,
And the bench provides them with comfort and good.

Yet no one remembers the old tree,
Its importance now long forgotten,
And though its legacy lives on with the bench we see,
The old tree's memory has been rendered rotten.

But let us not forget the gift it gave,
The shelter it provided through the rain,
For the old tree was once so brave,
And its beauty will forever remain.

Me and My Shadow by Rob Masson

I'm an Undergrounder - a Subway, Metro, Tube Type.

Some like trains with an overhead sky or boats or planes and some, God help them, love steering a car through traffic but me, I prefer being below ground. The shrink has leaped on this as the explanation for everything. I don't argue with her. If you've tried talking sense with a shrink, you'll know what I mean. But I'm not denying it. It's where my story begins - on the Coronation Line, the Beckham Boulevard stop on a Thursday evening after the rush hour had died down.

Thursday is Writers' Class. Story-telling is good recovery therapy for someone like me. The Clinic recommended it which was their polite way of telling me to go or else but, as it turned out, I enjoyed it. If not for my Thursday class there's no telling where I might have ended up.

Anyway, that night at the Boulevard she first entered my life, standing too near the platform edge in my opinion because you can never be too careful in public places these days. She was nothing special; pony-tail, baseball cap, knee-length black overcoat and a nice pair of legs in pink and white trainers. She had little plug-in earphones connected to her mobile phone and a bottle of Highland Spring water in the crook of her arm. Like I said - nothing special. Just what I was looking for.

Let me explain that last remark before you get any funny ideas.

I was developing the right frame of mind for my class. Take a window-dresser's dummy, baby-pink, just out of the box. Dress it. Give it a personality. Make it walk and talk. It's what we Thursday scribbling types do. So, I started with a name and called her Laura. She lives with her mum and dad in a semi-detached house in a dormitory suburb while saving for a deposit on an inner-city flat. She's very disciplined, willing to make short-term sacrifices. As a school-girl, she practised and practised until her little fingers were raw and bloody to earn piano certificates for Mum to frame and hang on the sitting room wall. These days she has no time for the piano but listens to Elton John and Abba on her mobile phone.

So, now that the doll walks and talks, what makes her clockwork tick? What's happening underground, Laura? How does it feel coming home to Mum in her rubber gloves fighting an endless battle against microbes and dirt? And what about Dad, ranting and railing against the television news, cursing the Houses of Parliament while Aliens in flying saucers and rubber dinghies land on Hastings Beach? Leave? I can't afford to leave, she moans while suspecting that's merely an excuse to cling to the nest.

Anyway, before I could get any further with her - ever have the feeling that you're being watched? I do. It was one of the reasons I ended up in the Clinic. I've learned to fight it since and my prescription tablets help when I remember to take them but that evening it was very strong, like a tap on the shoulder, a no-nonsense demand for attention and when I looked along the platform, I caught sight of him, watching me watching her. He was a square-headed, broad-shouldered, heavy-stubbled lump, in the Coronation Line uniform; baseball cap and overcoat, shoulder bag, water bottle and phone. But the peculiar thing about him, what really held my attention, was he glowed, not with health or happiness, not glowing with the light of love or the saving grace of Jesus but - darkly glowing. I know it's a funny thing to say but he appeared to radiate a cone of darkness around the station's arched walls rather than cast a shadow along the platform.

And he leered. He'd clocked me looking at Laura and no doubt, thought he knew what was in my mind. If Lady Gaga had been on the platform, a leer might have been in order but for Laura - sorry - not my type. I tried ignoring both of them, him and Laura and fixed my gaze instead on the tunnel at the platform end. The last thing I wanted was to be trapped on a homeward journey with a loonie but when I heard the train approaching I couldn't resist a look back. He was still there, with his stupid smirk and eyes fixed on me. He reached for the bag at his hip and patted it once, twice, three times with the open palm of his hand. That did it. It was like something from a bad dream that for some inexplicable reason can wake you with a cry of terror. Maybe it was nothing more than the air pressure being crushed into that small space as the train came into the station that made my heart race and the blood pound in my throat but, whatever it was, I panicked and wasted no time getting into a carriage as far away from him as I could.

I've always been an Undergrounder. I'm a primitive, I suppose, with instincts stuck in a distant past when our ancestors were some kind of insect - ants or termites. I'm compelled to go downwards away from the sun into the dark tunnels searching for the Queen's chamber, the heart of the Nest.

But, I'm not an addict to the Coronation Line. On free days it could be the Brexit or Olympic, any of the others that strike my fancy but during the week it's my way to and from work. For a few days, I put Laura aside and got on with my tale of the termite, lost in a rain-storm, trying to get back to the nest until one evening, homeward bound at the Boulevard, I caught a glimpse of a ponytail and baseball cap, a mobile phone and water bottle on the platform and the urge - the Laura urge - was rekindled.

Now, picture this – it's what we scribblers call the Flashback - we rewind some twenty-five years and Laura, wrapped in swaddling clothes or whatever it is that babies wear, arrives home from the maternity hospital to be greeted by a gang of goo-goo-gooing grand-parents, aunts and uncles and in that adoring circle, a space is cleared for her brother to get his first glimpse. He is three years old.

'Come and say hello to your new sister, Martin' says Mother.

He scowls at the mewling new arrival, clenching his little hands into fists.

'Take her back!' he snarls. 'I don't want her!'

That's it. Flashback over. Cut to the Boulevard where the electric sign announces an incoming train. I manoeuvre into a position where Laura and I can share a compartment and work on the next episode of Life with Martin. We rattle into the tunnel, strap-hanging, lurching from side to side, a little distance apart so that I can see her drop-earrings, like Christmas tree fairy lights. Back in time we go once again, Laura and I, to when she is nine years old, admiring the new outfit that Santa has brought her in the full-length hall mirror when along comes Martin wearing his Three Lions football strip. He elbows her out of the way.

'You look very nice, Martin' she says because she's a good-natured girl and the Yuletide spirit is in the air.

'What do you know about it ?' he sneers. 'You're just stupid, you are.'

'I'm not stupid! I'm top of the class in school. You're nowhere near the top of yours.'

'That doesn't mean anything. I could be top if I wanted but I don't because I'm the best footballer in the school and when I'm older and play in the World Cup and score the winning goal my photo will be in all the papers and Mum will put my winner's medal in a frame on the wall and you'll just be an ugly sister with sticking-out teeth!'

'I'm not ugly!' she says with tears in her eyes.

'Yes you are and you're skinny and ugly and no-one likes you so why don't you just go away? Go somewhere far away where me and Mum will never see you again!'

But then the train with a long screech of brakes comes to the next stop and Laura's a big girl now, grown out of her sticking-out teeth and skinny legs and the Coronation Line is crying out for girls like her, top of the class, school certificate girls. There are more desks for girls like her than places in World Cup Squads, Martin, and lots of schools and each one has its own best footballer.

Don't you go encouraging him with your football cup nonsense, Mum complains to Dad. He's such a wilful little boy. I don't know what will become of him if he doesn't get what he wants.

The compartment doors slid open and in stepped the Beckham Boulevard man.

He spied me, nodded in recognition and the leer spread across his face. The doors closed, the train started up and he took up position, legs astride for balance, leaning against the door. He wore the same outfit as the other night, baseball cap and overcoat, a chin of dark stubble and the canvas bag slung across his shoulder. We'd hardly moved from the station when he held up the index finger of one hand. Pay attention, it demands. He unbuckled the straps on his bag, and drew out what appeared to be a parcel, just enough for me to get a glimpse; a box, a pink-red oblong box but, only a glimpse and in such bad light that I couldn't really see what it was. He returned the box to the bag and held his finger to his lips as if pledging me to secrecy.

My first thought was that he was a suicide bomber about to detonate right there and then and had chosen me to tease with the knowledge that my last moments had come. He seemed so relaxed about it all, leaning back nonchalantly with that supercilious smile on his stupid face that I then began to suspect that it was a game he was playing, daring me to grab some railway cop and report this suspicious behaviour only to look a prize moron when the parcel turned out to be a birthday present for his girl-friend.

I couldn't afford that kind of fuss. I wasn't long out of the Clinic and still
on the tablets. The job wasn't much but it was a start. I didn't want to go back and begin all over again.

I watched his every move all the way to the next stop when the doors opened and with a little wave, not goodbye but I'll be seeing you, he stepped out onto the platform.

He was getting at me, this Coronation Line Shadow of mine. I liked saying that I was a Beckham Boulevard Investment Banker. I modestly claimed a back-room job and no-one needed to know that the back-room was the cafeteria kitchen where I washed dishes and humped sacks of potatoes. The job wasn't a stretch and nobody bothered me so long as I didn't cause trouble. The last thing I wanted was that my nerves snap and I lash out at him and the cops are involved. That Human Resource crew on the twenty-ninth floor have cut-throat razor eyes with smiles to match. They'd have me for breakfast - on toast.

But, for a few days things were quiet and I began to think maybe he'd found some other playmate on another line. My thoughts returned to Laura. I still had a lot to do on her story.

They pop up everywhere along the Coronation Line; there's a lot of her type standing too close to the platform edge. There's a swollen hive queen somewhere along the route spending all day making pony-tail and baseball cap clones for the nest. We've all got a bit of the ant and termite in us. I'm more ready to admit it than others.

That evening, in my usual spot, waiting for my train, I spotted a pair of bright green trainers and I had another Flashback. Laura takes after her mother; a kindly, compassionate girl, popular with the well-behaved circle of gold stars at school. Life with Martin is, however, a trial of kicks and punches and snarls and sneers but it serves her well, developing the stubbornness to succeed, the will to win. While Martin is in the back garden practising his Cup-winning goal dance or in his bedroom rehearsing his Match of the Day interview, Laura practises piano. Every Saturday morning she heads off to her private lessons with her sheet music in a Christmas present briefcase. Her piano teacher, a knuckle-rapping martinet, lives in a draughty house of echoes with her invalid mother. Laura holds her in awe but is not intimidated for under her bad-tempered tutelage she is making good progress. On one beautiful autumn Saturday in the suburban dormitory town, Laura rings the piano teacher's doorbell and –

A tap on my shoulder and my Coronation Line Shadow, as large as life, stands right next to me, overcoat buttoned to the neck and to exaggerate his oafishness, his baseball cap is set with the peak pointing backward. He carries the canvas shoulder bag. The leering smirk is on his face. He wipes his forehead with the back of his hand, sweating in the close underground air. He unbuttons his overcoat and lets it swing open. Beneath he is wearing a Three Lions football jersey.

He unbuckles the shoulder bag and draws out the pink box and holds it in the palm of his hand. I see now what it is – not a birthday present parcel in pink wrapping paper but a house brick, the pride of the London Brick Corporation. His smile broadens into a grin. His teeth are stained yellow.

He moves away with a jaunty gait, arm swinging freely with the brick in his hand, just like a clock pendulum. Laura stands with her back to us, far too near the platform edge as usual, earphones, Abba and mobile phone. I feel the rush of air from the approaching train and I realise what he intends to do. I try to stop him but he has a few extra paces on me and this is all he

needs. He brings back his hand and swings the brick. I hear the bone-crack as it makes contact with her pony-tail and I can feel the rush of blood from her nose into the back of her throat. She staggers from the blow and plunges onto the track as the train comes screeching to a halt.

Now hands are grabbing me and someone has me around the neck and despite my pleas the idiots let him get away. I catch one last glimpse of him merging into the crowd of onlookers, all those baseball caps and overcoats and shocked expressions. He gives a little wave of the hand, not goodbye, gotta go but I'll see you again.

They got it all wrong, cops, the shrinks, the lawyers, eye witnesses, judge and jury. No-one believed a word of my story. So, I'm in this place for a long stretch and won't be travelling the Coronation Line anytime soon and it's goodbye to the Writing Class. My shrink is very keen that I should keep writing and I have all the pencils and paper I need. She's not a bad sort for a Pony-tail and Spring Water type. She's very well qualified with a wall of framed diplomas in her office and likes Billie Holiday and Ella Fitzgerald though Lady Gaga isn't on her playlist. Her dad's a hot-shot in some top-knob University and Mum welds scrap metal into statues that she sells to people with more money than sense. The shrink is an all grown-up girl and unlike Laura has left the nest for a home of her own. She has Japanese prints of geisha girls on her sitting room wall.

But she's still a shrink and can't be told anything. I can't believe that my Shadow will leave me alone and the thought that haunts me is what he'd do if he found his way into a place like this. He's a Mad Hatter and this would be just the place he'd end up. Despite my best efforts she takes not a blind bit of notice and suggests, ever so tactfully, that I'm in denial. She'll be in denial if she gets a house brick cracking the back of her skull.

Anyway, that's my story for what it's worth. I've booked a seat off to watch the World Cup in the communal room after tea. The Three Lions aren't doing too bad but they won't lift the trophy. They don't have that key player to raise the team from being not-bad to being truly-great, the one who scores the winner in the final minute. The player the crowd loves. The player that every Mum could be really proud of.

One last thing before I go. Be careful standing too near the platform edge.

The Tankard's Mahogany Bar by George Fuller

Tom Cox

Bricklayer

With the Council

 Building Department

Got his hands

In Tavern Street

On *The Tankard's*

Mahogany bar

Grain reddish

Brown

Cut down

   Tree

Of Amazon

Over which *Tolly*

Brewery pints

Were drawn

Since the foul

   Crimean War

Dawn

Smooth worn

For Tom's cabin

Cruiser dream

Seating-scheme

Tom's sixteen feet

Of Amazon

Freed by Town
Planning
Demolition
Order
And wheeled
Fleet feet
To his tram -
Terminus street
End of terrace
Home
With mudflats
View
Balanced
On his bike
In the Year
Of Our Lord
1962.

Tom's eldest
Glennis was
   Thirteen
Linden he
Was middle
Next came
Gwyneth
Welsh named
All
By Mrs Cox

With love

For her South

Wales Women's

Land Army

Bosom friend

Arianwen

The *Tankard's* bar

Of fine timber

For Tom's

Double-ender

Clinker built

Larch-on-oak

Twenty-eight-foot

Ex ship's lifeboat

Where

In stern-post

Of oak

Was carved

The name of

Mother ship

Scrapped

Tramp steamer

S. S. City of Stoke.

Ol' Tom sawed

The Tankard's

Bar in half

Made two side
   Benches where
They all sat
Including Stan
A family friend
And bow-wave
Proud they cruised
Round the
   Estuary's
Dog-leg bend
Propelled by an
Old Austin 10
Car engine
Lead patches
Tacked on
The hull
Leaks
Preventing.

Cormorants dived
And seagulls
Screamed
At the noise
Of the rampant
Dream

O'Tom, he gave
His all

Finding timber
For that boat
Nowadays
They're all
Made of
Fibreglass!
So kiss my
Smooth and
Shiny
Arse

The Tulip Thesis by Michael Frank

Gordon is shy. Deep within, behind his moustache and his heavy eyebrows and his heavy large brow, is a bulb he uses as a storage device. It contains all his good stuff. His bright red colours. His father and mother are Indian and he feels the tulip resembles the turban his father wears.

Gordon does not wear a turban. But he remembers his bulb, deeply hidden, waiting for Spring to emerge and show bright red. Gordon arrives early to work and lets himself in through a non-descript door and follows the dull corridors to his dull office, his large, open-plan space, with its technical area that has glass partitions from waist to ceiling, piled high with equipment and projects and books and tangles of wires and old machines and old dust and new post and in-trays and out-trays and old phones and more cables and charts and all the things school lab assistants need.

Old coffee mugs sit beside old ash trays, where the cleaners don't venture. Where he is glad they don't venture. Where no one ventures. Where he can huddle by one ring of the electric fire and prepare to respond to all the usual requests. Where he can wheel his trolley loaded with a VCR and a television to the third floor on Wednesday afternoon for Open University Mathematics: Theory of Vectors. Where he can manhandle a huge chart on population for the old-fashioned Statistics teacher who never changes her syllabus year in, year out.

It is Monday and Gordon is tired, but happy. Happy to be sitting, alone. Happy to have managed to hustle some sort of breakfast, happy to be here, to be earning some sort of points by arriving before anyone else in the department. Soon bells are ringing, feet are shuffling and Gordon brings his huge forehead a little lower and finds something to pretend to be engrossed in.

Unusually, there is something in his 'in' tray. His stomach starts to churn. Dark thoughts enter his mind, rushing past like images on the old-fashioned duplicating machine, making him think about going to the toilet, making another coffee, reading a book, preparing his first presentation for English Literature. He fiddles with a trolley, takes out his schedule and checks what they need. OHP. Nice. Transparencies. Wordsworth. Poetry. Tintern Abbey in 1794, a watercolour by J. M. W. Turner. Wow. That's cool. That will look great projected on that big wall on the second floor. He would have to get up there early and black out all the windows properly, like Leget never bothered to do. Leget would moan of course about it being totally dark, but Leget was so lazy. If Gordon made sure the lights were on before Leget arrived he wouldn't even notice the blacked-out windows. He could even take up that little lamp on the trolley so that idiot could read his notes from the trolley. He got out the folder and arranged it. He lost himself, preparing the trolley meticulously.

He even convinced himself the letter in his in-tray was a good thing. It made him focus on work, on what he knew. Not these stupid new initiatives from the school board. Or complaints. Or cutbacks. Or restructuring. He didn't love his job, but he had settled in. After four years, he had grown comfortable. He felt his bulb growing fat. He felt he was developing, getting ready, strengthening. So that when he decided what to do, what he wanted to do, he would be able to launch into action. Or at least to make a slight improvement. But life was going well. He planned to move out of his parent's place anyway. That would be a huge move, for him. Huge. Bolstered with all these self-congratulatory thoughts, he decided to take out a notebook and pencil, and deal with the letter.

Gordon loved 'troubleshooting'. It was a technique he used for everything now. He found it so effective. He originally came across it when doing a PC Servicing course. His tutor, a marvellously non-communicative Italian guy, who was always head-down in 'the next class', the 'next project', so he never had to deal with what was in front of him (i.e. a student), strangely came alive when confronted with a problem. For example: a dead computer. He had this method. He would always shoot into action, logically, methodically strip down the machine, rebuild it, and get it working. But he always knew what to do, never hesitated, never got upset. Every next time the machine failed to start he'd just go 'bing!" next procedure. One day he let Gordon in on the secret. He outlined on a piece of paper, as Gordon was now doing, a table with 3 columns – problem, cause, solution.

Maurizio (that was the name of the IT tutor) never seemed to get excited about this process like Gordon did. And sometimes Gordon wondered what other secrets Maurizio knew. Perhaps, deep down, there was a slight sparkle in Maurizio's soul. It was hard to tell, as most of the time he was bent over the machine, banging a chip or wrenching out a cable. But Gordon got a thrill every time he drew that table: problem, cause, cure. Once that was done, he felt he had caged the wild beast that was the new problem.

He had invented his own variations on the method as well, which consisted mainly of tables which could refer to other tables, each with their own page in the notebook. Gordon always thought of Einstein at this stage. He was reported to have said that 99 % of a problem was analysing the problem. Gordon knew deep down that Einstein never said this. But somehow it comforted him. He was being like Einstein. And the idea seemed to work, regardless of any genius's involvement. So, thought Gordon, pencil in hand, what's the problem?

The letter. That letter. He wrote that down on a new page in his new notebook and read it back. 'The letter'. He drew a table with lots of rows and three columns. Problem, Cause, Solution. He left it blank for the moment. He brainstormed ideas on a blank page. He paused and got on with other tasks. He set up another trolley, nodded to people as they wandered into the main section of the lab to pick up a coat or a piece of equipment, or to answer the phone. After a few minutes he actually wanted to do the brainstorms so he returned to his notebook and let his brain run wild. When this brainstorming eventually dried up he filled his table with ideas about the problem. He got into intricate detail. He moved onto the next column: cause. Why did he have this letter? He rattled off possible reasons:

To tell him something. To tell him to do something. To ask his opinion. To give him bad news. To give him good news. He exhausted every possibility.

Finally he tackled the last column: solution.

For each cause he came up with a solution.

He took another break. He came back some minutes later and scanned his list of 'solutions'.

The overriding 'thing to do' became 'read the letter'. It recurred throughout the list of solutions relating to different causes.

That became his solution. Read the letter. He would appear to have got nowhere. But. He felt in control now. He had analysed the situation. There were no stray thoughts on this problem. He had gone deep. He had gone subterranean on this problem. He was dealing with it. And how long had it taken? Not long, not long at all. And he had wasted no time fretting, worrying. He was in charge now. He could justify himself.

He went for lunch. Happy with his mind, filled as it was with one instruction. He was even starting to be positive. He had dealt with things like this before. Life was good. He plonked down the tray in a battlefield of spilt coffee and used paper napkins. He didn't care about the hygiene of the canteen. He loved the canteen. The simplicity. He worshipped the simplicity of it. You came in here, you sat, you ate. Simple. His colleagues sat nearby, then fellow-technician Jason came over and sat next to him. Unusual.

"So?" Jason says. Stranger still. He was talking. Jason throws down a letter on the table.

"What do you think?"

He was still confident the matter was in hand, but a few fears rushed in and out of his mind as he dipped into the baked beans and toast. Fears and Tears. Fears for Tears. Did they know the similarity? He felt his eyes moisten – but that was a good thing, wasn't it? Moist eyes? He opened his eyes wider and directed his huge blank forehead and heavy eyebrows down onto the letter, but blurred the words because he knew Jason had read it.

He would let Jason explain.

"This is it! This is a total assault on the department! A rebrand, a restructure! Out of nowhere! No warning! Nothing! This is insane! What are you going to do?"

"What choices do we have?" asks Gordon, hoping he won't have to read the letter. Jason must have worked out their options. He had.

"Well, redundancy can be good." It didn't sound good. "Or transfer." Erm....not great.. "... or just hang in there".

Now that was the option that attracted Gordon.

"Can we do that?" he asks.

"Well..." Jason attacks his egg with a dirty fork, "... in theory. If you wait it out, do nothing....accept the job description changes.... in reality a lot of this stuff in not applicable. I mean, in reality...."

"It won't actually happen?" asks Gordon.

"Well, yeah, it won't happen, in fact. In reality. But it will happen on paper. "

"On paper?" says Gordon.

"Yes, on paper. Which means it counts when you go for your next job. It counts on your CV."

There was a sluggishness to institutions, an entropy, which Gordon loved. This is what drove most people mad, but to Gordon it was just fine. That was his ace in the hole. He was not clambering for change, reform, efficiency. He often appreciated the status quo. It was a reality to him. The nonsense, the long way of doing things. He thought it was like nature. Nature did things the long way, the proven way, the ridiculous way. Gradually. Slowly. He could incorporate that into his daily schedule.

Jason was growing wearisome now. Gordon felt he had obtained a lot of information from him but the effort to keep talking was annoying. He dried up and thanked Jason, who moved back to where he usually sat and started muttering to the rest of the department. Gordon was still quite happy to ignore the whole thing till he got back to his office and his notebook.

He started filling up his table cells with little tasks. Open the letter. Good. Small task, specific. Decide where to store letter. Scan–read the letter. Make notes on the letter. Analyse the letter. Re-read the letter. Record yourself reading the letter. Scan the letter with the camera. Project the letter on the wall. Photocopy the letter. Put a copy of the letter on the wall. Highlight key words. Glean all the information from the letter.

He had learnt that official letters like this contained a deceptively vast amount of information. He wrote down names, addresses, telephone numbers, made notes of all references to 'for more information', contact......He made a file for this letter. He would have all the people, all their contact information in that file. He would research the department. It was amazing how much information you could find out about a department with just a few phone calls. They even produced pamphlets, sometimes. You could gain access to their mission statement. Their goals. Valuable information. Empathy. This was Gordon's version of empathy. He saw the letter as the result of a long process. Someone had composed this official letter. This was the end of a long process of gathering and presenting information ... it had value.

It also had a message. It had impact. He had to determine what this meant for him. Personally.

He saw it as a good opportunity to understand his own position. He looked up his original application for this job. His job description. He looked up his contract, all the personnel guidance, letters, information. It was all fuel to his defence. Ammunition. Hard information. He put it all in the file. He saw where he stood. He had never done the job described:

"To be a conduit for the easy flow of technical information to non-technical staff at the institute." Specifically: coaching, teaching staff on technical issues through presentations to groups and individuals.

Usually, he would deliver equipment and the teachers would use it. Now, it seemed they were going to get him to teach them how to set up and use the equipment. They would be collecting and setting up the gear. How would that work? What would he then do? Well, that was where the restructuring came in. They were cutting staff. He would, if he stayed, have to take on four people's work. But this was all analysis, speculation. Gordon got back to his notebook and read the letter.

Immediately, it seems, he did not have to decide anything, but the letter told him to look for a communication about a presentation he would have to give to the Art Department teachers. Were they trying to kill him? A presentation? To people? A room full of people? Did they want him to quit? Was that it?

The 'communication' came through in the form of an internal memo. He had seven days. Seven days. The worst. He would have to think about this. A presentation. To people. Speaking. He was not sure his voice could even hold out for.... how long was it? Details. That's what he needed. Buried deep in the 'communication' was a 'more detail' and a 'help' number and name and department information. He checked his file to learn about this department, this number, this person.

He needed to see the contract, as it were, the small print, the terms and conditions that no-one read. They were his friend. This he could deal with. Text. Small print. Conditions. Exceptions, excuses, rationale. Reasons. This was his leverage. He realised after half an hour he was enjoying himself, and he hadn't even drawn up a table for this new 'task'. Quickly he started a new notebook and headed it 'Give a talk'.

He enthusiastically analysed the problem. This he could do. He would find a way. Talk without saying anything. Like a politician. He would be present – undeniably present – without doing anything. He would make them waste time. He would find the parameters and all the excuses to make it shorter. He would employ imaginative techniques to do the talk in the most oblique way possible. He would make them talk! He would have an extensive 'q and a' section. He would make them fill out forms, all as part of 'his talk' time (this might be fiddly but he could ring up that help line and

concoct some reason why it was essential they answer a lot of questions). He would stall, prevaricate, speak as little as possible. He would write out a speech and get it put on an auto-cue of his own design. He would make them get him a glass of water, as soon as the clock on his speech was ticking.

He would not answer their questions. He would make it a 'brainstorm'. He would write their questions on the chalk board – after spending a long time cleaning it. He could play music! Surely, he could play music. He could show a film. Surely he could show a film in a talk on Art!

He needed to rehearse. That took time. He knew this, but that was all stuff he could do alone. He could enjoy that. His empty days became full. He was building his suit of armour. He worked it out. His speech would consist of one hundred words, maximum, with no direct interaction. The rest of the time he could be fiddling with equipment, scraping tables noisily across the floor, waiting for malfunctioning equipment to begin working, writing down their questions on the board. He would be alright. He felt alright. It was alright. For now.

Days like these, (no-one told me)
by Frances Ogiemwense

I fold my lips up into a smile

For people who ignore me

I fear that I haven't fought hard enough,

For people who adore me

I weep without shame to a stranger on the phone

When Secretly my heart has snapped, like Cracknel

And I'm sitting here alone

I swear I will lift the sword of righteous wrath

Against the goliaths of hate

If only I could find the strength again

If only the world would WAIT

Uncle Bob – or – My take on religion, by Dave Chambers

Part 1

Saturday morning was catechism class, we'd all turn up at the chapel to be schooled in the art of being a Catholic, not just a Catholic, a Roman Catholic. All that means is a bunch of other Roman Catholic boys around the same age who lived in Cupar – a small town of just over three thousand people, would walk down the street then turn into the little close and walk the few yards to where we could gain access to the chapel. Roman Catholic places of worship were not allowed to have an entrance directly from the street, but were forced to have 'back doors', (that rule, law, was changed in 1966).

It was there that the nuns instructed on the things we needed to know so we learned all about the ten commandments, including the bit about going to Hell if you break any one of them, and die before you get to confession and the priest gives you absolution so your soul is clean.

I didn't get the bit about coveting next doors wife or coveting other stuff that other folk had, but there was one that was really easy – Thou shalt not kill! Simple. Easy instruction to obey - who or what was I about to kill, nobody, nothin', no trouble I'll be all right, I didn't want to kill anything – but there was one terrible flaw in my thinking. When we left that day, and wandered up the street to where a couple of the lads would go into the ice-cream shop and the rest of us would walk on quietly coveting, for me, this particular Saturday was different.

'Thou shalt not kill' was ringing in my ears as I carefully inspected exactly where my foot would not step on an ant, or any other small creature that might be using the bit of pavement where my shoe might land. The others
were looking down the road – shouting 'What you doin?' and laughing their socks off when I told them, but I persisted.

So much for the easy one… The most simple commandment, easy? Simple? Who said that?

I do have to confess that the odd sausage, or mince and tatties, or 'bone for the soup' that Mum occasionally managed to get from the butcher's shop did not give me any sense of doing anything that might be wrong. I just didn't think that far.

Well, right now, I'm talking about November 1947/48 and this particular Saturday was a good one because it was the one where my Mum would take me with her on her fortnightly afternoon visit to St Andrews and I'd see Granny and Granddad, and then we'd walk up the street a bit and we'd see Mum's brothers and sisters, most of my cousins and in particular, Auntie Daisy and Uncle Bob.

He was my favourite Uncle. He always had time to look at whatever I had to show him, time to listen to my latest adventure. I just liked being in his company. And one of the most vividly clear memories of my childhood happened on one of those visits. It was a few days before Armistice Day. I would have been five or six years old.

"Where's Uncle Bob?" I said brightly.

"He's in the bedroom, getting ready for the parade," Aunt Daisy said.

"It's not today," I said, incredulous at the thought of him getting ready a few days early.

"No," she laughed, "He's just making sure everything's all shiny." She must have seen my puzzled look, for she went on, "Go in and see him and ask if he wants a cup of tea." I was puzzled again. Why did she just not shout like she usually did? The house was like ours, not that big. But she insisted, "Go on, ask him."

So I went, pushed the door open and walked into the room.

"Uncle Bob do you wa..." I stopped and my mouth fell open.

He was standing quietly in the small room staring at the bed. On it was a dark suit laid out, and a regimental tie. He was not looking at them. His gaze was fixed on a large piece of felt laid out at the foot of the bed. I can still see them, a row of medals glistening in the light from the back window. I felt my eyes growing with every second.

"Uncle Bob," I almost shouted, "What did you get them for?"

He jumped, startled, then with one flowing movement flicked the cloth over the medals and growled.

"For killin' men." I had never heard him speak like that before and have never heard such anger in anyone's voice since, 'For Killin Men' a simple statement, but so powerful, so angry, so regretful, so sad, all at the same time.

The medals made a thump as they dropped into the small wooden box that looked just big enough for them. The anger in his voice had startled me and I wished I hadn't asked. I felt despair at my Uncle's anger. I didn't feel that he was angry with me, and he did not look a bit like the hero in the comics or the films or the Pathe News when we saw some General in uniform with a chestful of so many medals we wondered how he managed to stand up and we cheered so loud no one heard what was being said on the occasional Saturday matinee. No proud accolade here.

'For killin' men'.

They were men, not Jerrys or Ities or Japs. Not even The Enemy. They were men!

I thought about this, but didn't tell anyone, never put it into words, not until a few weeks later at the Saturday morning catechism class I was sitting on my own and one of the nuns came and sat down beside me.

"You've been very quiet for the last few weeks, has anything gone wrong? She spoke softly and sounded quite concerned.

My bottom lip trembled as I said – quietly, out loud for the first time "my Uncle's going to Hell"

"Why do you think that? What on earth has he done?" She sounded shocked.

I struggled for the words "He's killed men."

"He's killed men?" She looked truly shocked, "How do you know he's killed men?"

"He told me."

"He told you?"

"Yes, he told me, and I saw the medals."

"Oh!" she sounded relieved, "He won't be going to Hell. That was wartime. That's different."

"*NO IT'S NOT.*" My reply was immediate, but not out loud, not even to one of the kinder nuns. However, my mind was made up. Well, no it wasn't, I had to think about it a bit longer.

Does all that mean, if we had lost the war would Uncle Bob end up in Hell, and all the Jerrys, Ities and Japs would be sent straight to Heaven? Confused is not a good enough word, not by a long shot. Just didn't sound right.

That's where my real doubts started. I still continued to attend every Saturday, I still took care when walking along the street, but didn't make such a show of it, so apologised and said a (silent) prayer whenever I thought I'd made a mistake.

Part 2

Some years later, at the secondary school, when we were taught more about the history of our world. About the Conquerors, Kings, Emperors and 'leaders of men' who throughout history had brought the world to where it is now. Empires came and went, we always seemed to know more about the winners, and how the losers had made mistakes. The losers were 'the baddies' so we always knew which armies had lost wars and gone to Hell, and which armies had won wars and gone to Heaven.

Of all of the ancient empires that have gone, did the soldiers who built the empire all go to Heaven, and only the last ones who lost the empire go to Hell?

Sounds a really stupid question, probably is one of the most really stupid questions ever to be put into words, but it nagged at me then, and even now, when I'm an octogenarian, it still nags . . .

A progression through the ages of things that happened long ago and how we British built a great empire, gloriously touching all the lands, and all the seas, and all the oceans in the world: and as we were the winners, all of our guys went to Heaven – well, as they say – a pinch of salt, or a bucketful, would not go amiss.

So, I still could not be satisfied that Uncle Bob would get to Heaven because we won the war, surely there's more to it than that, Some Generals, or other leaders, sign an 'armistice document' and one of them is sending all his lost/dead troops to Heaven – the other guy–? ? ?

I think I just did not believe that nun, but I never dared tell her.

Part 3

My education progressed through multiple different phases, but there was a constant, that religion, the 'wrong one' could get you in a lot of trouble – mostly dead. Whether that got you to Heaven or Hell kind of depends on who wrote that bit of history. If you're a 'devout' person you've a good chance of getting to Heaven, otherwise, well?

Then there's the local Baron whose wife has given him a series of daughters. The wedding ceremony has that phrase – 'no man shall put asunder' – so there is no such thing as divorce, but the available solutions are, arrange an accident, she could fall off a horse, or he could Mount a Crusade.

Gather some of the men that he owns, arm them with pike staffs or bows and arrows, or clubs – not swords, they're not gentlemen, give them some training and with much pomp and circumstance, march off to 'The Holy Land' and while there, pick a fight with whoever is not a 'Christian' and make as many of them dead as you can. When you think you've got enough you gather all the men you've got left and come back home, and on the way take a detour to Rome, meet with the Pope and boast of your killing spree in the Holy Land, and if it sounds good enough the Pope can annul the document saying you are married, and you come home in triumph, kick out the 'single woman and her now illegitimate female children, choose a new wife who would, hopefully, bear a son. And if necessary, do it all again – and again, maybe not, they'd be too old.

Meanwhile, the estate, with most of it's workforce absent for a few years, is not in as good shape as it was before they left, and to get things back to a state where they can grow enough to feed themselves, the peasants really have to work hard, to make up for that part of the workforce who didn't make it back. They, of course, would all be in Heaven.

Other religions have their own history, some of which is still being written and some things we hear (if we hear correctly – which is not a given) do appear to have equally questionable routes to Heaven.

The above is just the thoughts of an old man as he looks around the world at how religions are being presented to us from day to day, each one being advocated as the religion which is the true saviour of mankind, often losing the fact that a 'woman' is also, by definition, another man . . .

I have not *studied* religion of any sort, and have no thoughts on making any attempt at persuading anyone to change their religion or question what their teachings have told them.

This is simply the ramblings of a crusty old man so you don't have to take any notice of any of it – not one bit of it, or change any of your thoughts, ideas, ideals or beliefs.

If you feel you should do something - and if you have a mind to – perhaps – you might say a prayer for me?

Thanks for reading this far, and in anticipation of any intervention you may make on my behalf . . .

So, I decided not to follow any religion. If I'm wrong I'll go to Hell, and taking into account what I've already said above, I guess that means I'll be going to Hell, with the losers. So I guess that's where I belong.

On the other hand, thinking about it, I guess I'll be more at home there.

RESIGNATION by Catherine Daniel

I love you

With bared soul and open heart

I love you

With all that is good in me

Loving to a depth profound

Where wisdom cannot reach

Without limit, condition or reservation

Such love does not need proximity

Or communication, to flourish

Nor seeks response or acknowledgement

Of a love that will endure

From near and far

And will not fade or change

This side of eternity

Mission To Zelba by Paul Germain

In another universe there had been a great war, between agents of Lanar the Light One known as Xedo Protectors and agents of Duzur the Dark One known as the Graul. The two sides possessed the Xed Element which manifested physically as a shining liquid material contained in a bracelet. The Xed Element granted powers to the user such as extended lifespan, sensing other Xed Element users and more. The Graul had won the Great War.

Relgo, a young Xed Element user had been assigned to Xedo Protector Yadorn Vezlo for training. At a later stage, the pair were chosen for a mission to the hidden world of Zelba to locate and retrieve the legendary Armour of Huldoo. The elder Xedo, had spoken for years of the armour. Forged by the Huldoo of old, the armour could amplify the powers of a Xed Element user. It was by luck that the location of Zelba had been revealed. An ancient technology built inside the world allowed it to shift instantaneously to different locations. A vast holographic field kept the planet hidden from view. It would shift at regular intervals.

Yadorn waited by the small triangular starship in which Relgo and herself would travel. The ship had wings at the upper back with thruster engines at their centre. Yadorn was of athletic build with flowing purple hair. She arrived early that day and was keen to undertake the mission.

A gentle rain began to fall as Relgo arrived on his R42 Light Bike, which consisted of a metallic base with a shaft upfront leading to handlebars. It hovered over the ground. Relgo was a jolly type and of slender build with spiked dark hair. He set the bike controls to 'rest' and dismounted.

"Well, I'm ready if you are," he spoke.

"Good to hear, Relgo. Let us depart," replied Yadorn. The two boarded the ship through the rear hatchway and sat in the control area. Yadorn contacted Algar the eldest Xedo, on the ship's computer. Algar appeared on the rectangular energy field which acted as a screen. "We are ready to leave. We'll soon have the armour," said Yadorn.

"Be careful, and may the Light One go with you," came Algar's reply.

Yadorn initialised the take-off thrusters and the ship rocketed skywards. She input Zelba's location to the computer and set controls for hyper light. It would take four hours to reach Zelba at its current location. Once there, they would have two hours to locate the armour before Zelba once again shifted.

Yadorn meditated. Relgo went to the cargo-hold and practiced combat techniques, returning later to the control area to meditate also. The computer sounded an alert to confirm destination reached. Although appearing to be in deep space, the duo was aware of the holographic field as Yadorn took the ship forward. There was an electrical disturbance around the ship, and then before them lay Zelba.

It was a small world with two continents, one a desert, the other mostly forest. The Xedo had learnt that the armour was in the forest continent where an ancient Xedo meeting place had also been located. Yadorn landed the ship in a clearing near the meeting place. As they landed, unbeknown to them, another ship that had followed them, made ready to land.

Yadorn and Relgo made their way on foot to the meeting place. It was a circular area of ground with smoothed tree stumps as seats. Yadorn stood centrally as Relgo playfully jumped from stump to stump.

Yadorn advised Relgo, "don't underestimate Xedo incantations. Once learnt they can boost proficiency with the Xed Element."

"I'll continue my studies on that," replied Relgo.

"The darkness of the Graul grows as we speak," continued Yadorn, "I feel the armour is nearby. It will grant unquestionable power. We leave now," warned Yadorn.

The two entered the dark woods. "What was Graul Prime like before the Great War?" Relgo asked.

"Universe Central, as it was known, was the shining jewel in the universe. I would often visit Morr's café," replied Yadorn.

"And your favourite dish was...?"

"Oh, that would have to be the UC Burger Deluxe. Very tasty!" Came the reply.

"I wish I could try one."

Suddenly, Yadorn placed her arm in front of Relgo.

"What is it?" whispered Relgo.

"Darkness is descending. We must proceed carefully," replied Yadorn. A terrible shrieking of horrid creatures became audible. The woods grew darker. The duo covered their ears and stumbled onwards becoming separated as they wandered further apart.

Eventually Relgo saw a shaft of light coming from a clearing. He pushed his way through some thick foliage and headed over to it. Once there he found the armour shrine. He was about to move nearer when an imposing Graul warrior stepped out as if from nowhere. "The armour belongs to Zordak," he growled, referring to his leader, and shot shadowy beams from his Xed Element at Relgo, which the young man narrowly avoided.

Yadorn appeared, "Run Relgo!" she shouted and attempted to shove Xorl the warrior with a light ability, but it was repelled, sending her flying. Relgo stood frozen with Xorl advancing, then calming himself, loudly spoke an incantation: "Armourrorro!" With that the armour flew from the shrine and attached to his body. He raised his arm skyward, the armour shining brightly.

Xorl stood ready to resume his attack. Relgo shot a wide light beam from the armour enhanced Xed Element. The beam destroyed Xorl's left arm at the wrist. Xorl roared clutching the injury as he retreated. Relgo held his arm aloft with his Xed element darkening and crackling with energy as did his eyes. Yadorn shouted. "Stop Relgo! Remember who you are!"

Relgo paused. His eyes lightened and he collapsed. Yadorn hurried to him. "It was taking over," panted Relgo, "Duzur is powerful."

"With further training you'll learn greater control. Now we must hurry to the ship before more Graul warriors arrive."

The two returned to the ship, blasted off and headed for home.

On the Central Line by Andrew Diamond

(Narrator is a lady on her mobile phone returning from work)

We've just arrived at Leytonstone, I'm sorry it's so late,

The journey's been horrendous, get the dinner on the plate.

I had my lunch with Tracey, she was temping in the Strand

And the money she was earning was pro rata thirty grand

But her governor, who was married, said he liked a bit of rough

And when he tried to touch her up she left, she'd had enough.

There's a new bloke in our office and he's trying to impress,

But he's gobby and his hobby is to stare right down my dress.

The geezer sitting opposite is ogling my boobs

And if he doesn't watch it I might kick him in the tubes.

Look, I'll phone a little later when we get to Newbury Park.

You can fetch me from the station, save me walking in the dark.

I've been doing data entry, it's been doing in my head,

So after we've had dinner let's have pudding up in bed.

More Tales of Glo and Laura by Ros Allison

Well, I can't write that.

I can hear the deafening silence from the rest of the class as they all drift into a coma while they try to pretend to be interested in the life of an ordinary housewife. That gangly guy sprawled out next to me, legs and arms looking like they don't want to be confined to a chair, seems bored already. He looks like he has already made his mind up that nothing being read out by this class would hold any interest for him unless he has written it.

All I've managed so far is: 'My name is Laura, I've been married to Alan for thirty four years and we have two children, Alice and Guy.' So, that is going to blow their minds!

What we should consider, according to our temporary tutor Sharon - call me Shaz, everyone does - is that nobody wants to hear our parents' names or which school we went to, and we should keep our job history for our CV. Apparently, what we all want to know about each other is what makes us, 'us'.

What Shaz should consider, is the length of her skirt, if she's going to perch on the edge of her desk like that. But I'm not her mother, and comments like that would just get me one of her exaggerated eye rolls from Alice - and I am her mother.

Hopefully, when we get to meet our real tutor, Michael, who Shaz is standing in for - no explanation given - he might come up with a more interesting subject to get our creative juices flowing.

So, next week I've got to tell this class what makes me 'me'. God help me! I've got no idea what made me, 'me', not sure I even know what it means. I think I just happened. Isn't that what we all do in the end? Start out with some fancy notion of who we are going to become, and then just become what we eventually are? I know it's very fashionable these days to tell kids they can be anything they want to be. But, really? I mean, good luck with that. You might just find out that what you want to be is not entirely in your hands. Like the rest of us did - well, those of us who aren't Madonna and the like.

God knows what the schoolgirls Glo and Laura thought they were going to be. Not sure we had a single ambitious thought in our heads. Too busy partying and drifting in and out of increasingly more inappropriate relationships. Having fun, getting drunk, being young.

When I met Alan and we had a family, nobody was more surprised than me at how much I just fitted into the role of homemaker and mother and wife. Actually, that's not true. Glo was definitely more surprised than me. She still finds it fascinating all these decades later.

When she called on Thursday to change the arrangement she had made the day before about Saturday night, and Alan had to call me because I was hoovering - she couldn't have been more confused if he'd just told her I was dancing naked on our garage roof.

"What the hell, Laura? You were hoovering when I called yesterday! Please tell me you don't hoover every day?"

"No Glo, only when it needs doing. And just in case you're interested in my regime - which I know you aren't - I was hoovering downstairs yesterday and upstairs today."

"There's only two of you! What the hell goes on in your house that makes you need to be hoovering the whole time? Does Alan walk around spreading crumbs all over the carpets from the constant stream of pastries and cakes he stuffs into his mouth everywhere he goes?"

"Yes, Glo, that is exactly what happens. That is a perfect description of how Alan behaves. We live like pigs. And of course, there's always the evidence of all the cocaine I'm snorting all day long that I have to hoover up in case we get raided by the drug squad."

"Thank God for that, it all makes sense now. For one horrible moment, I thought you actually liked hoovering."

So, if even my friends and family think I need therapy, what chance have I got with those two earnest-looking young women - possibly Dutch, but I'm hopeless with accents - who arrived in class first, just ahead of me, and sat at the front. They are surely not going to settle for anything less than novels worthy of a Booker, even if only in their own opinion. They are around Alice's age, but I would be willing to guess that the similarity definitely ends there.

I'm drifting off subject, as usual, and need to get back on track with trying to pretend that my life lends itself to writing something that would sound interesting - which would be the definition of creative writing, now I come to think of it.

I suppose I could write about that horrible bloody cruise that Glo tricked Alan into booking. The only good part was that I managed to persuade him that we couldn't go away for the four months he had impulsively signed us up for - I had the opticians and Alan would lose his slot with the chiropodist, etc. So, he managed to get a bit of a refund and booked four weeks instead.

Why the hell anyone wants to float around looking at the ocean for weeks on end beats me. Alan got some sort of horrible bug and ended up in the hospital bay for a couple of days - which was fun for me. Then he couldn't shake off the unwell feeling for the rest of the cruise and spent most days just sitting on the deck. There wasn't any energy in him, which is unheard of normally. Thankfully, he had packed some books and he likes reading
but doesn't often get the chance, so it didn't seem fair to disturb him.

Anyway, the offering of activities like fruit carving and napkin folding didn't seem to appeal to him. Can't think why!

Of course, with bugger all else to do - off I went. And the only thing I learned from all that effort is that I have no aptitude for fruit carving or napkin folding. My pineapple owl looked like the cat had got it and I couldn't have put the napkin creations I crafted on a dinner table without looking mad.

Some of the dance classes were ok, but I only went when driven by desperation, because I don't like being partnered with someone I don't know.

The entertainment was hit and miss - mostly miss. And just to add to the whole uplifting experience, a couple, who frighteningly don't live far from us - a fact that Alan couldn't keep from them despite the 'look' I was trying to fix him with - seemed to have us under surveillance or security tagged, because every time we sat down to eat, there they were. It was impossible to lose them, whether we ate early or late and whichever of the eateries we chose, the mousy little Deirdre and her ghastly husband Des were at our table in minutes.

*****

Deirdre is probably younger than me, but dresses like my mother. And Des, who has the look of the sort of man you wouldn't want to get alone in a lift with, always managed to sit opposite me and did his best to impress me with suggestive eye contact, and the sort of false wit, charm and flattery that just gives me the creeps. Do women really fall for that crap?

One evening, Deirdre tried to be subtle as she dug him in the ribs for staring at my cleavage. "I was just admiring Laura's rather lovely necklace," was the best he could come up with. When they'd left and we were finishing off our wine and coffee, Alan, who was the only one at the table who didn't know what was going on, commented on it being strange for a bloke to admire necklaces like that. Alan's never been the jealous type. I don't think he would have noticed if Des was on the floor looking up my skirt. I wouldn't have put that past Des either.

Anyway, there must be something I can use from this experience to make me sound interesting. Maybe I could write about how Alan and I are intrepid travellers and say something about all the countries we have visited this year already. No need to mention that we were on a cruise.

And I could list carving from natural materials and origami as two of a long string of hobbies if I leave out the fruit and napkin bits. In fact, what the hell, I could say anything.

'My name is Laura, but my alter-ego is Chartreuse Devine, when I appear on stage as a Burlesque dancer in private members clubs all over the country/world. I met my husband/lover? when we were working as undercover agents for the British government, in covert industrial espionage assignments.'

Now, that is more like it. I could actually start to enjoy this 'writing about me' lark.

By the time Saturday evening arrived, I still hadn't made a real start on my writing assignment and I was feeling the pressure of having to produce something to read on Tuesday. But we were out with Glo and Brian in a local restaurant, and the evening was very full as usual with good food, plenty of alcohol and the sort of light, easy conversation that comes with friends we have known forever. To top it all, Alice popped in to join us for coffee and it was a while since I'd seen her.

She announced that she had had the sudden impulse to bake a batch of ginger cookies during the week and was seriously worried that she might be

turning into her mother. So, Glo said she would round up some of her girlfriends and go round to her flat to stage an intervention. They didn't even care that I'm sitting there.

So when Sunday came 'round, I was really feeling the pressure about this piece for the class, and I had spent the morning shopping with Steven, who wanted me to help him choose a birthday present for Guy. Steven's great company and we had a really fun morning. I feel so lucky with Alice and Guy - and Steven, Guy's boyfriend, is a bonus. Alice, at 30, still shows no sign of slowing down or settling down with anyone, although baking cookies is such a departure that anything seems possible.

I had probably had one too many gin and tonics with Steven to settle down and write my story for the class, and I was a bit too excited to sit still because he said something that made me feel like they might be getting married. He didn't actually say that, but it was the impression I got, although when I told Alan what he said, he was less than convinced and told me not to get carried away. But I want to get carried away, so that's what I'm doing.

And with all that going on in my head, it was obvious that the writing muse was not going to be upon me, so I took myself out to do a bit of gardening for an hour.

Just as I was putting things away in the shed and getting ready to go back to writing, the neighbours came out - and they were rowing. Properly rowing, loudly, in their garden, and there was some very personal stuff being bandied back and forth.

It was obvious that they didn't know I was there, and I didn't want them to think I was listening, so I just stayed in the shed, thinking it would all blow over or continue back in their house before very long. But it didn't blow over. In fact, it blew up. Even their families were brought into it, with him telling her what he really thought about her mother and then her retaliating. And so it went on. I certainly learned more about them than I ever wanted or expected to know - and I couldn't get out of the shed, could I?

Even when Alan came out and called me I managed to keep quiet, but then he went back into the house and called my mobile, which has a very loud ringtone and rather gave the game away. Now, I had to come out of the shed with my phone pressed to my ear so that I could get back into the house without having to do anything more than a cursory nod in their direction.

And by then, of course, it really looked like I had been listening. I had to do what Guy calls the 'walk of shame' down the garden and past them.

The whole experience was unsettling and time consuming, and by the time I got back indoors it was time to get started on dinner.

So, it was well into the evening before I got a chance to log on and get this damn piece about me out of the way, and I still didn't have a clue what I was going to write.

Then, I got a WhatsApp from Glo. "Saw this poster in the library window when I was out with the girls for lunch, and it seems like the sort of crap you would love to waste your time on, so I thought of you." The poster was advertising a class in stained glass and Glo was absolutely right. This is exactly the sort of crap I like to waste my time doing, so I called the number straight away.

A very nice lady called Marion answered, who didn't invite me to call her Maz, or come across as someone who wants to flash her knickers to the class. She said the class started last week, but they had just been talking about equipment and introducing themselves, so I hadn't missed much and nothing I couldn't easily pick up. I enrolled there and then.

I called Glo straight away.

"What the hell were you doing in a library?"

"Are you kidding, I wasn't in a library. I haven't had a library card since I stopped having Bunty, I'm not you."

"I can't remember you ever getting much use from a library card, and I'm quite sure you never read Bunty. You were nicking your mum's Cosmopolitan to bring to school when we were still in primary so, how did you see the poster?"

"I was standing outside the library, waiting with Sarah while she had a fag."

"Oh right, that makes sense now."

"You should have come, we had a good time. Mel's got a new man in her life who sounds like a riot. They were all asking about you, but I told them you were probably scrubbing the kitchen floor or running up some more cushion covers, or whatever the hell floats your boat these days."

"I was out with Steven, as you well know, and we also had a really good time."

"Are you thinking of joining that bloody awful sounding class then?"

"Already joined."

"You are a lost cause."

"Well, stop trying to save me then."

So, I'm going to learn how to make stained glass.

Sounds right up my street, and I am really looking forward to meeting Marion and getting started, but what's even better than getting a new opportunity to start learning something I know I am going to love is that that class is on Tuesday nights - the same night as the writing class. So now I don't have to do any creative writing. They will all have to manage without hearing my scintillating life story.

I think a stained glass light shade would look lovely in the stairwell.

A Thousand Tongues by Mark Altenor

"A picture paints a thousand words"

A quaint familiar phrase

is oftentimes interpreted

in somewhat fewer ways

The maxim says succinctly

with considerable gall

what many would agree with

and seems obvious to all

It states the tongue just cannot tell

of wonder like the eyes

But that's not the entire tale

or where the real truth lies

One word can say so many things

another one, exact

The key is in arrangement

that's a fundamental fact

A thoughtful word, a chosen term

a speech that is Churchillian

A thousand "illustrative" words

are worth a common million.

Fin.

A Southern Aspect by Nicola Catton

I was waiting for the elevator at the St Regis Hotel New York, this may have been one of the fastest cities in the world, but the ride up was real slow. My demeanor sure changed when I saw a familiar face approaching, he didn't know me, but I knew him. He was unassuming, kinda regular but interesting, wearing slacks, a shirt and a smart but casual jacket. He was carrying a fancy pen that he was clicking occasionally, just like he had a burr in his saddle. Well butter my butt and call me a biscuit, it was Paul McCartney.

He stepped nearer to the elevator and looked up at the numbers getting lower. It was at this point, as he settled into the spot next to me, we briefly made eye contact. 'Hi' I said and gave him a dumb smile like I didn't know who he was. 'Good afternoon' he grinned. I pretended to look into the air around me, not being bothered by his presence. Secretly I was flapping like a mad goose, gee this is a story to tell the grandkids. I was never really a fan but some of their music was sympathetic to the rhythm and blues that I grown up on.

We entered the elevator, he gestured for me to go first 'Thanks' I said, still acting as if he was just a regular citizen of New York but accepting his British gentleman courtesy. We stood silently for a while, giving my noggin time to think. There was one thing I longed to know about the Beatles. Should I ask him? This will be my only chance, arr shit or bust.

I hadn't got much time, although the elevator was traveling slow, I needed to act fast. 'Hey, I'm Maeve' I said 'Can I ask you a question? 'Hi, well, sure' he answered with a weak Liverpudlian accent. I think he was taken aback by my blousy southern approach. 'I've always wondered about that Something video, it looked like you all had really made it. Like you were all living the life you dreamed of, you all looked more... individual, what do you think? Am I right?'

'WOW, that was such a long time ago. I remember filming that because I looked pretty manic, with the beard and crazy eyes, I was with Linda at the farm. I think we were just coming to the end of recording that album and I was exhausted' rubbing his chin, pondering the answer 'I suppose we had made it in a way. We'd come a long way from the back streets of Liverpool and our working-class upbringing. Even, a long way from the American tours and the matching suits, which were cool at the time I might add.' Pointing his finger up, raised eyebrows, animating the point. 'But yeah, we all could afford to buy things and it gave us the space to develop as individuals. We'd grown up I suppose and found love. John was with Yoko; George was with Patti and Ringo was with Maureen. If I remember rightly, Ringo had been traveling in Europe.'

'Exactly, he had that European je ne sais quoi, particularly the hair' I interjected 'Really, ok yeah, I can see the hair now.' Paul responded 'You know, we all filmed that video separately, at our own homes. We'd become more accomplished by that time. It gave us freedom.' splaying his hand whilst tucking the other under his arm. 'The freedom to do what we wanted, be who we wanted, learn what we wanted. It gave us artistic license; we could say what we wanted, however we wanted. It was also the beginning of end, you know.' Again, pointing but wagging this time 'But we enjoyed the ride.'

Ah, this is my floor now, I'm sorry I've got to go, it was lovely meeting you Maeve and I hope I answered your questions' 'Yes you did, thank you so much' I said 'Y'all have a good day' and he was off waving his way out of the elevator. I eyed him down the hall until the elevator doors started to close. What the heck, I slammed the elevator doors open and held them.

'Hold your britches, what do you mean the beginning of the end? Was ya foughten' I pleaded. He sighed and smiled 'No It's just that It wasn't long after that that we officially split up.' talking while walking backwards 'We'd

already stopped performing live and concentrated on recording in the studio' his voice getting louder as he got further away. 'When did you last play together? He stopped, hands on hips, facing me, right sad looking 'It was on top of the Apple recording studios, we played Get back among other songs.' head hung low 'Except, we couldn't go back because we didn't belong there anymore.' He took a pause and breathed deep 'I'm sorry Maeve I can't answer anymore questions, I've got to go.' Off he took, my eyes fixed. Well smelly clarkson... the demise of success, huh.

Driving to Work with a Stowaway
by Mandy Grainger

Triple check the door's locked.
Did I pick up my phone?
Go wash your hands again.
Have I smudged my lipstick?

No one hates the skittering insect that lives in my brain more than I do.

Where is my phone?
Did I send that work email?
That fucking song again...
What's this guy looking at?

It trills and wriggles at random, and sometimes it burrows down deep.

Shit, I missed my turning.
Does my cat know that I love him?
I wonder how many years I have left.
That's a pretty blue.

It delves in from the outer periphery into the dark creases of grey matter,

I'm pretty sure she hates me.
Who the fuck are you kidding?
Why are you even trying?

No one gives a shit.

It finds a fleshy morsel to gnaw on for a while just to keep me subdued

You're an imposter.
You're a child.
You're lonely.
You're ugly.

Then – temporarily sated – it leaves a small void behind as it scurries out again.

You're a failure.
You should just give up.
No one will miss you.
Or your bloated face.

Sometimes I think about squashing that bug against the wall. Hard and fast.

The Worst of Times Part 1 by Frank Crocker

Both my Grand Mothers had passed away by this time, (1962), and whilst I got on well with my paternal grandmother Katy, I have to admit, I do not remember feeling any great loss, or sadness, and even wondered if my feelings were lacking in some way, especially seeing other members of the family upset.

I was twelve when my Uncle Phil died, after a long battle with lung cancer. He was, as I mentioned before, a heavy smoker, but nevertheless, he died at fifty seven, which was sad for the family.

I still never shed a tear. I carried on going to school, playing with my friends, watching the Flintstones, reading DC comics etc.

My Mother asked if I wanted to see Uncle Phil's body in his casket at the undertakers, and I insisted that I did very much want to do that. My parents gave each other a look, and asked if I was certain, and I told them he was my favourite uncle and that I definitely did.

On entering that cold room where his body lay, what I saw shocked me, not in the sort of shock that makes you jump out of your seat, like in a horror film, but it was definitely a physical feeling. Rather like you get as you drive over a humped back bridge a little too fast, or as you hurtle down the descending slope of a big dipper.

This lifeless body that I was looking at, was a grotesque caricature of that funny, charismatic, Irish-American that drove me around in his blue and white Ford Zephyr, and white-walled tyres, whilst teasing me mercilessly.

What I was saw was someone whose handsome features were now, sunken and hollow. His shrivelled body gave him the appearance of a plucked emaciated bird of prey. My lasting memory though, was his cold yellow waxen skin. Even Madame Tussaud's chamber of horror dummies, to me, could not match that harrowing cancer-ridden skin tone.

My feelings as a twelve year old were confusing. Whilst I was unable to shed a tear for my favourite uncle, I distinctly remember seeing my father one morning, wearing Uncle Phil's dressing gown, and experiencing a feeling of disgust. To my logic at the time, it just didn't seem right. *it was Uncle Phil's dressing gown not yours*!

But my opinion of "grown ups" was about to sink even lower, because Phil had formulated a will that would distribute his estate equally to all his brothers and sisters, *except* his brother in Texas, namely Tim.

Maybe every family has an Uncle Tim, "flash", overbearing, the sort of individual, so pleased with himself, that he would have happily drank his own bath water. He sometimes wore silvery mohair suits, with massive lapels, along with eclectic ties, with intense technicolour yawn patterns. Sensible brogues or casual Hush Puppies were never going to be found on Texas Tim's feet, only correspondent shoes, or cowboy boots, polished to a mirrored dazzling shine. No self-respecting game show host would have worn outfits so loud. He immigrated to the U.S. but settled in Houston Texas, where one presumes they actually accommodate, even foster, delusional imperious gentlemen of that ilk. I spoke to my sister Mary, and found out that he was also a groper. Indeed, he accidently on purpose brushed his hands over her breasts on a couple of occasions when she was sixteen and on her trip to the States with my Mother years before, so all in all, he was a premier league sexual predator.

My Mother, Paddy, and her four sisters May, Romana, Hilda and Kitty all thought it would be a good idea to distribute the estate uniformly to all the siblings, *including* my Uncle Tim.

Tim, so I am told, refused this compromise, and said he would not accept charity, and from what I have been able to gleam since, set about a chain of
events that only profited the legal profession, and, inevitably, saw the worth of Phil's estate dwindle and disappear like an empty promise.

Two years later, when I was fourteen, Kathleen, his (Tim's) wife flew over to Britain, perhaps it was a sort of diplomatic charm mission, to heal family divisions. Kathleen was an American. She was slim, and in her youth was very attractive with a peaches and cream complexion that the Texan climate, before the days of factor 50 sun screens, soon sun-dried. She had a gentle nature, was softly spoken and mild mannered.

One of life's puzzles really, how on earth this beautiful woman, in her day, could have fallen for Tim, an uncouth "gob-shite", pint size, Irish chancer?

Kathleen brought with her, Maureen, her adopted daughter, who even without ever having met her, I was doggedly prepared to dislike.

*****

Maureen was a U.S. citizen, born in Ireland outside of wedlock, to, I suppose, a young Irish girl. As was accepted practice during that period, such was the shame of illegitimacy that babies born into that condition would be handed over to local nuns, in this particular instance, the "Sisters of the Sacred Hearts of Jesus and Mary".

The Catholic Church, during that period, oversaw Social Services and Education. Children born outside of marriage would be absorbed into the Church orphanage system.

Uncle Tim and Auntie Kathleen went to Roscrea in Tipperary in 1951 and purchased Maureen for an undisclosed sum, from the sisters. About four years later, Uncle Tim and Auntie Kathleen went back to Roscrea and this time came away with a baby boy. Only the price had doubled. Boys were more expensive.

This system of exporting unwanted children to childless couples around the world, but particularly the U.S., must have provided the Church with a welcome income.

Recently, within the grounds of this particular Orphanage, they found the graves of an unknown number of Mothers and babies, named without irony "the Angels Plot".

It seems that every year that passed, further scandals emerged about institutions such as these. In Roscrea, at this location, 1024 illegitimate children died over a 37 year period.

Even accounting for Maureen's ignorant adopted father, she was fortunate to have been whisked away from Roscrea. *In many of these homes, the children that survived often suffered from "marasmus" which was a form of severe malnutrition. A child with marasmus looked entirely emaciated with protruding ribs, and body weight was reduced to nearly 60% of the normal body weight for the age. Children in these homes were dying of starvation one hundred years after the famine.* The Irish Star

*****

So, there I was, stuck with this American girl of fourteen, with teeth in braces, freckles, blue eyes and fair wavy hair. I had convinced myself, that she was going to be the "spit" of her adopted father. A "know-it-all motor mouth", topped with an awful Texan drawl. It is said that some Texans have such an unhurried manner of speech, that by the time they finish telling you about their past, you are part of it.

Well! The facts were this. She did have braces on her teeth, she did speak with a Texan drawl, she did have freckles and blue eyes, and after a short while in her company, I thought she was just glorious. It was as though we had known each other all our lives. It was full on Puppy Love.

The summer holidays were here, and my given duty was to escort her 'round London, which she was quite fascinated with.

She was a huge fan of the Beatles, and really impressed that I could hammer out "Twist and Shout" and "She Loves You" on the piano - in quite a rudimentary manner. We wondered around, hither and thither, for about a week, and I was intoxicated with her. One lovely sunny afternoon we stretched out on the grass on Parliament Hill, and she asked if I had ever kissed a girl. I hadn't. She told me that she hadn't kissed a boy either, and at that moment, we should have joined lips. I could feel the tingle from her breath, we were *that* close, but, neither of us could actually go that extra half an inch, and, well, kiss.

We did make a solemn oath, however, to meet in New York when we were nineteen.

Her holiday in England was over, and she and Auntie Kathleen were going to Ireland, then back to the States.

Two days later, my Mother came up to my bedroom first thing in the morning, as I was just approaching consciousness, and took my hand, very gently, and told me that Auntie Kathleen and Maureen had been involved in a car accident on a road in Tipperary, and whilst Auntie Kathleen's injuries were not serious, Maureen had been killed outright.

I cannot remember if I cried, but, I had a new experience which involved an eruption of herpes-type "cold sores" around my nose and mouth!

There is a certain mocking irony I think, that this gentle creature died in the county and country she was actually born in.

Eco Friendly by George Fuller

Wheeled through the back
Gate on a gleaming sack
Barrow – my new electric cooker
Solar, wind, and nuclear
No carbon emission
Like the old gas issue
£25, second-hand in '92
Down the Romford Road
Now bound for the scrap-yard
Flat in the back
Of the fitters van

The flat before
Was fourth floor
And she cried:
"But I've got a baby!"
But how could he lift
A cooker up
Eight flights of stairs!

It used to be
Kindling and coal
Town gas and paraffin
From coal mines, pipelines
And Persian Gulf tankers
Pylons and power stations

And now we've got wind turbines and solar arrays
Mighty wind turbines and solar arrays.

Customer Service by Michael Frank

Martin looked at the people in the train and walked along. No space, no space, no space, no space... No mask, no mask, no space, no space... The noise sounded. The doors were going to close. He slid on through the door and decided to stay standing. He looked around. What could he do? People were too close but this was it, this was people. There was no logic to them. They were just stupid. And there were too many of them. Ah... the distance in actual reality was more like two feet than two metres. Were they exaggerating how far you had to stand apart? Did they think if they said two metres people would keep two feet away? And what they actually wanted was for people to keep two feet away? Mind you, Martin didn't really mind avoiding people. It was his natural tendency anyway. Why would he want to get close to people?

The train rattled along, then got into its screeching mode as it went round the bend. Ear-piercing. He thought about putting his headphones on. The ones that enclosed his ears and protected them. But no, he wanted his wits about him these days. It was amazing how much sound helped. You know what people are like, with their phones, staring at their phones, headphones on. Oblivious, bumping into you. He didn't want to be one of those sheep, one of those morons. One of those idiots. It was only a few stops. Here it was. Piccadilly Circus. What a nightmare. The busiest station. He liked it though. It was autumn. It was cosy, it was warm. It was circular. He zig-zagged this way and that. Avoiding the morons with their headphones and their phones. Their eyes not working, their ears not working. Their brains not working. They were working, though. That was the thing: these were the cream of the crop, these were the people who were working. These weren't the unemployed, these weren't the beggars. These were the cream. They were awful.

He climbed the stairs. And hit the pavement. To be met immediately by some beggar, who had no regard for social distancing. His sad eyes looked at him. Ill-kempt hair. Dirty, blue rucksack with a hood on his anorak. "'scuse me, 'scuse me, 'scuse me," he kept repeating, "scuse me, scuse me". Ah. Martin had caught his eye. He had not been prepared. He didn't know what to say. He didn't really mean the guy any ill but he didn't know what to do. If he gave him money, would the guy just spend it on alcohol or drugs? If he gave him money and he spent it on a cheese sandwich, would that really help him? It was depressing. Martin felt depressed now. The guy wouldn't shut up. "Excuse me, excuse me". He wanted to engage him... in conversation. It could be anything. Maybe he wasn't a beggar. What was he supposed to say? "Excuse me, excuse me, excuse me."

"What?" Martin said, against his better judgement.

"Ah! See....You're the first person to talk to me. No one talks to me."

I wonder why, Martin thought, but he didn't say anything.

An aggressive loud noise burst into his ear drums. A police car. Trying to speed along but no one letting him through. So he just revved there. Siren deafening Martin. Now he had to listen to the guy's story. "Yeah you're the first person... Thanks mate, you're the first person who's stopped." Martin realised he had stopped. Why had he stopped? "Yeah, you're the first person. No one stops. You're the first person who's stopped today – listen mate, look, look, the thing is, listen mate, the thing is..."

You're not my mate, thought Martin.

He started fishing in his pocket for money. Was he insulting the guy? Did he want something else? What if he was lost in the city? He would want
people to stop and talk to him. He had been poor himself. He'd travelled. He'd reached the end of his tether. But he was on his way to work. He was late. This was stupid. He wished the guy would get on with it. He fished in his pocket and he couldn't find any change. He thought about reaching for his wallet and then he just lost his temper and snapped.

"Look mate," he said, "you've got to be quicker than that."

Moving on, Martin was again met head-on, this time by a woman, carrying a baby. "No, no, no," said Martin as she started talking.

Her big dark eyes filled with tears, pleading, "my mother, she come, my mother she come, please, please."

"No, no, no," said Martin, turning to the right.

He was sure he had read they were all in gangs, the national costume provided and the babies rented. He couldn't give to them and support that terrible trade. No, you had to be cruel to be kind. Don't encourage them. Buy the big issue. They are licensed. They are genuine. They are trying to improve themselves. Mind you, they used to piss him off. They never gave him the correct change. He wanted to demand it off them, then tried to explain he was not giving them money, they were running a business. Every other business gave him his change. "You have to get a hand up not a hand out," he told them.

"I've been doing this 18 years," one guy told him. He was young, tall, able-bodied, quite literate sounding. For 18 years? That was not right. It was meant to be a stop gap, not a career. In the end it was just annoying, and he resolved next time he came out to come ready, armed with small change to give to them and move on. But how? He didn't want to put it in their hands. He wasn't shaking hands with his family so why should he get so close to these scumbags. No. He thought. Sorry and all that, but it's tough times. Get a cup and I'll drop all my crappy loose change in. They were barely human

anyway. They did not appreciate the finer things in life. Snot dripping from their noses. Dirty beards. Spitting in the street, shouting, drinking, vomiting... they were hardly human... and who's to say they didn't choose that life? And if they did, well fair enough, he wasn't going to insist they were locked up. But they were asking, and he was saying 'no'. They had the right to ask. And he had the right to say no. Or did they? Wasn't begging illegal? Why have laws if you don't enforce them? So you can enforce them when you want to. When someone is subversive. It's social control. Police state. Martin believed in the law. He thought laws should be enforced or be abolished.

Once he'd made his mind up, he felt happier. Then this guy in a light green suit spoke to him.

"Excuse me, old man," the voice was frail, delicate, but sort of relaxed. The voice of privilege, but then it changed, "old bastard, init! what eh?" then back to the public school: "You see the thing is old man," and then, "bloody hell, you sod. Sodding hell."

What was this? Martin looked again at the suit. Now he saw stains, brown, white, the dust sort of sat on him. His shoes were nice, but he had no socks. Public schoolboy, alcoholic, drug addict...

"I knew Jimi Hendrix you know," he said and pulled out an album by Don Cherry – at least it was the sleeve of a Don Cherry album… "Want to buy this? Classic. Beautiful. Five pounds is all. Mint."

"I don't have a record player," said Martin.

"No, no, of course not. Want to buy a watch? What? Not half, bloody hell. Fanny on it. Gorgeous. Look. Bottle of Stout?" He offered him a sip.

"Sod off," said Martin, then, "thank you, I gave."

"Yes" he said as Martin brushed past, "yes, I gave. A pint. An armful! Tony Hancock. Bloody hilarious. Old wanker. Old sod."

Martin pushed the door of Slaughterbones then remembered it was automatic. Down two steps and into the safe haven. The unemployed. Invisible signs said, 'no beggars, no unemployed'. Only the cream in here. The employed. The gainfully employed. Those with homes. No homeless, no gypsies here. Independent people here. Decision makers. Those in charge at least of themselves. Those taking care of business. He breathed in that air. A fresh air. Eau de cologne. His own. Others. Women with perfume, men with deodorant. Yes, he breathed it all in, the smell of vape coming from the staff room that he now entered.

Martin slid around like a fish in his aquarium. Not talking. Feeling loose and slippery, disconnected. He carried books. That centred him. But did it really? They had atomic weight, sure, physical weight. But did they ground him? Were they not themselves just bubbles of thought captured in words? Aren't we all just captured here in this earthly form? Maybe he should have been grateful he could think.

Then he thought of the stupidity and the laziness of it. He spent hours, he spent his life, putting books back on the shelf. It was like filing. It was slowly wearing him down.

'No,' his positive self pops up, which is odd for a positive self! But no, it has more to say on the subject: 'It is good physical exercise! Imagine being chained to a desk all day! You are keeping fit! You are lucky to be working in a book shop!'

He moved this way, sliding, gliding along the floor in the warm air on the fourth floor until he realised at 11 o'clock he was making a noise. He was muttering. He stopped, then found himself doing it again ten minutes later. He decided it was time for a break. He was due a break. He had been working for two hours. He made his way to the cash desk but then realised, as he mumbled 'why can't they put the books back?' under his breath, that he should really put these away first. Otherwise, where could he put them? If he just dumped them anywhere he would be no better than THEM.

He could not hear birds singing in the staff room. There was only him and the hum of the air con. There was only supposed to be one person in here at a time. Bloody Covid. He loved it. All this solitude. He realised, he said this under his breath as well. Why did he live in London if he hated people so much? He didn't hate them at a distance. He hated them close up. Two meters (which actually translated into two feet), seemed ample close enough for Martin.

Martin thought about taking off his mask. He was alone. But... he was supposed to keep it on. So he did not spew out germs. If he had germs. He had not been tested. The tests were pretty hard to get and pretty useless. He thought they are like women in this respect. Not really worth the effort. He would wait until they worked better and were easier to get. When would they be easier to get? When he had a better salary and a better flat. In fact, what woman would refuse an offer to dinner at a nice restaurant then back to a lovely central London flat? Besides, he was intelligent, not too ugly facially or bodily.

The thing he misses, he supposed, was seeing people's expressions. He loved being able to hide his face, but really, without that eyes/mouth, mouth/eyes response, bodies became even more meaningless and lumpen. What could he read from body language? It lay too much on the voice. He never trusted the voice. It needed the eyes and mouth, it really did. Mind you, like Hilda Ogden taking out her rollers, taking off the mask outside was such a joy. It did make life somehow magical. Like a Zen master now, though, he had to 'guard his senses'.

In the shop they had taken out all the seats, to stop people sitting down. Like everything else in this crisis. Such a unifying word that, whereas in reality there is no unity. For God's sake, there is no crisis, except death, which there always was. It is a mass hysteria, not a crisis. Everyone suddenly realising they are going to die. How immature, how bloody immature. Did they not realise this before? Did they not realise your granny dies; you die? We all die. It was a media hysteria – the best kind. The politicians just responding to whatever front page screamed the loudest. Populism. Great.

Everyone's a policeman now, he thinks, as he looks at the CCTV images that sit above a small bookshelf in the staff room. He sees some guy in a stupid blue anorak, with, inevitably, a stash of books under his arm, wondering around looking for chairs by the big low round table in the philosophy section. He had some crappy sort of self-help books with him. The wrong section. Great. He'd have to trudge all the way over there.....Oh God, what now! He was, oh no, he was sitting on the floor! He plonked down his books on a pile on the table and now was sitting on the floor cross-legged like some idiot hippy! Jesus!

"You can't sit down," says Martin, when he makes it back to philosophy, "because of Covid."

The guy stands up at least. From the mask comes some angry words which Martin can't make out. The guy bends to his book, which he is reading. But he is not only reading, he is bending the book back.

"Excuse me, are you going to buy that book?"

The guy turns around, shocked, thinking the interaction was over. "No, I mean, I may. I don't know."

"Well we can't sell it if you bend it back like that."

The customer is amazed.

"Are you still talking to me? What are you talking about? How come you can sit down in a cafe? Do you have a set of regulations I can read? No, seriously, you should have a book of all the things I have to do when I am

in your shitty bookshop, so I know how to behave. Like is it ok if I take a shit, right here, on the carpet? Is that ok?"

Martin is shocked. "No" he says, "you cannot behave as if you were at home..." and walks away. The guy follows him to Sartre.

He is mumbling something under his breath now. Maybe it was the masks that did it. He searches for a place to put 'Nausea'.

"What's your name, you asshole?"

Martin knows how to wind this guy up. He calms himself. "I am afraid it is store policy not to give out names."

"Don't you wear little badges like good little corporate slaves?"

He peers at his polo shirt, looking for a badge.

"I would kindly ask you not to bend the books back..." says Martin, noticing the guy is still holding the book in the same way.

"Yeah, right. So. What's the number? I want to complain about you."

Martin leads him back to the till and spends a good few minutes looking up a number and writing it down.

"You're about as good at doing that as you are at doing everything else. You know I support this shop. I am the customer. Your boss will be very interested to hear how you treat customers."

A Run around Mount Tamapalais
by Frances Ogiemwense

In the wind, leaning past conversation
lower than footsteps
stretch the wires of tumultuous emotions
there, other people's heartbeats take the place of voices
Souls rampage in the deserts of life, trailing colours

Contact is necessary for normality
the natural restoration of vision.
The sturdy thighs of morning time
Waiting in relief before the slopes,
trained to pause,
Waiting for the extremities of life to pass.
Those platitudes of peace, only liars in time.
Grotowski's day, beautiful open Theatre
There is no final curtain here.
Scribbled dreams pass as life

Old man, sat in the Pheonix flame
On your last afternoon you hold onto love.

In The Café by George Fuller

It was early
Empty nearly
When I said
To the Turkish
 Looking lad
"A mug of tea
And a crusty-bread
Sausage sandwich."
And he said
"That is £3.50."
I put three
Pound coins
And a fifty pence
On the counter
And he said:
"Perfect!"
As I saw in the
Paper rack
A Mirror – not just the Sun
Thank Christ.

And had just sat down
Reading about our
Duke
When six police came
Through the door

In a hurry

Made me worry

But I ain't done

Nothing wrong

Five boys, one girl

In blue

Four white, two black

Clattered down

At the next table

And I chirped:

"You had me worried for a bit!"

And one

Turned and said:

"Yeah – we worry a lot of people."

The cops: they're alright these days…

Farewell by Shah Obaid

"They're gathering," my new colleague said, looking at me.

"Oh yeah, let's go," I replied as I locked the computer and walked toward the hub. I could hear the chatter in the open hub.

The hub was an open breakout space used for lunch breaks or informal company gatherings. Silver-haired people occupied most of the chairs. Those leaning against the side walls or pillars were rarely talking. I stood at the end, just straight opposite him.

Now I could see his wrinkled face, framed by a shock of white hair. I could feel his bittersweet emotion and sensed his pride. Sitting on a high red stool adjusted to its maximum height, he appeared still, but I knew his hands would tremble as usual.

The Managing Director honoured his three decades of career growth from intern to Senior Manager.

"He's been a role model in our company. I can't thank him enough for his services."

During the speech, I fixed my eyes on him. He seemed to feel proud of every appreciation, his face blushing and his lips twitching. It was as if he had fulfilled his life's mission.

Today, I looked at him. I tried to look into his eyes, though I couldn't see his blue eyes from this distance. But at least today, I could stare at him without looking weird. Everyone was looking at him. No one would suspect me or catch me wondering why I was staring at him. It was his big day - his lifetime achievement day.

I had never stared at someone for that long in my life, not even my wife, when she was asleep. Today, everything felt different when I looked at him.

"And now, I want to invite him to say a few words…" the speaker announced.

I sneaked out and darted to the washroom. It was empty. As I stood before the washbasin, I caught a glimpse of my blurry reflection in the mirror. Outside, I heard the faint sound of footsteps. I rushed into a toilet cubicle and waited, but no one entered. I came out and looked again in the mirror. This time, my reflection was clear and staring back at me against the backdrop of the commode.

Returning to the office floor, life resumed its usual pace. Everyone was in their seats, fingers clinging to keyboards. He was also at his desk. I didn't know what he was doing on his last day in the office.

"Oh, here you are. I didn't see you there," the new colleague said, turning around in his revolving chair.

"I got a phone call."

"Alright. Have you seen him crying?" the new colleague leaned toward me, speaking in a low voice.

"Crying?" I inquired.

"Yes, it was very touching. He became nostalgic and mentioned that the office was like his home…"

"Ah, of course, he spent almost his whole life here. Isn't it?" I replied.

"He'll receive a generous retirement package. Plenty of money… He should be fine."

"I hope so. But do you think money is everything?" I pondered.

"But he'll have a peaceful future ahead. That's what matters now for him."

"Have you ever considered wanting to be in his shoes?"

"What do you mean?"

"Imagine if you were in his position, and today marked your retirement day…"

"No…no way."

"Why not?"

"I do not know. But I want to enjoy and fulfil my dreams…"

"Don't you believe he has also enjoyed his journey and pursued his dreams?"

"I do not know. We all have unique paths."

"True," I agreed, turning my attention back to my computer.

"Are you coming to the pub for farewell drinks?"

"Maybe."

"Oh, come on. I know you don't drink, but join us for some fun. And it's Friday."

"Ok. I'll come, but I won't stay for long," I replied.

As the clock struck five o'clock, everyone began packing up, heading to the pub. Glancing at his empty chair, I realised he had already left for his farewell party. I finished my report and emailed it to my boss, knowing it wouldn't be read before Monday.

I stood up again and looked around. This time, the entire office floor was empty. While my computer was shutting down, I stared at his empty chair. Considering the limited interaction I had with him during my two years in the company, perhaps my farewell to him would mean nothing. Still, I made my way to the pub, ready to bid my last farewell.

The alleyway leading to the pub was crowded, resembling a swarm of angry, buzzing bees. I lingered with some of my colleagues. I saw him inside the pub with several other senior managers. His eyes carried the weight of a defeated gambler who had lost everything, as he left the casino empty-handed. The mere thought of such a fate revolted me, leaving me torn
between feeling sympathy for him or harbouring scorn.

Just then, I felt the vibration of the phone in my pocket, disrupting my thoughts.

"I can't hear you... Hold on a minute," I excused myself from my colleagues and walked away.

As soon as I turned the corner, I hung up on the nuisance call. I took the bus home. Today, I didn't pick up the evening paper or read a book. I just looked out the window.

"You came early today. Is everything okay?" My wife looked at me in surprise. She was busy preparing dinner.

"Yes, I'm just a bit tired," I replied.

My daughter jumped from the sofa and ran towards me, wrapping her tiny hands around my leg and resting her head on my knees. I lifted her into my arms and gazed into her eyes. They were full of life.

"You seem troubled. What's the matter?" my wife inquired while serving dinner at the table.

"Nothing," I replied.

We had dinner quietly. Only our little one was the one we were busy talking to while eating. After dinner, I switched on my office laptop and opened my mailbox. There were several unread messages from this afternoon.

My eyes fixed on one particular email, which detailed my upcoming annual appraisal meeting with my manager. Uncertainty loomed over how long I would continue in my current job. Leaning back in my chair, I contemplated my next move.

"What is it?" my wife questioned again.

"I told you. Just fatigue," I replied.

"I don't think so. Something is bothering you."

"It's just the office workload. Can you make me a coffee, please?"

While she was away, I started typing an email. In the subject line, I wrote "resignation." Then I started typing. Once I finished, I read it again. But it was awful and sounded dumb. I deleted the entire text and tried again. This time, I simply wrote some generic reasons, like the company not valuing me as a key employee and being unable to afford to live on this salary. I reread it a few times. By the time I was clicking on the send button, my daughter cried, and I rushed to the living room. She had hurt herself with some toy. I bandaged her hand and sat there with her.

When I returned to the computer, I realised it had run out of charge. Oh no, I had forgotten the charging cable at the office, postponing the resignation until Monday.

On Monday, I walked into the office with a renewed sense of purpose. I knew it wouldn't be easy, but I was determined to make a change. I felt a flicker of excitement for the possibilities that lay ahead.

As soon as I sat in the chair, my manager asked me if I could have the appraisal a bit early. We proceeded to the meeting room, where the familiar pattern of intimidation ensued. I received minimal recognition for my efforts to secure a promotion. However, I received a small raise.

Without uttering a word, I returned to my desk. My laptop was now fully charged, and upon signing in, my drafted resignation email popped up on the screen. My heart raced as I read it once more. With no further hesitation, I clicked the send button.

Within minutes, I received a message from my manager requesting a meeting later that day. But what more could we discuss?

Throughout the day, I didn't cross paths with my manager. Finally, with an uncharacteristically wide smile, my manager arrived. We proceeded to the meeting room. My decision was final - I was leaving.

"Look, I know you deserve better, and you are one of our valuable team players. I am proud of you and your performance," my manager began with an unwavering smile. "Today, I fought for you with higher management. You will be pleased with what I am about to say. We truly need you in the team. You will be promoted, and your salary will be increased accordingly. What do you say?"

"Oh…really…thank you. I don't know what to say," I stammered, disbelief washing over me. However, doubts about my initial plan crept into my mind.

"No worries. Take your time. I will email you all the details. Review them and let me know what you think."

As I rode the bus home that day, a tempest of thoughts and emotions swirled within me. The following morning, after deep reflection, I surrendered - but with a promise to fight back soon. From my new desk, I now had a close-up view of a bare scalp, crowned with strands of shimmering silver hair, its owner now claiming the empty chair.

Misspent Youth by Mandy Grainger

I remember looking up at the night sky

Watching smoke dance with memories and regret

Then I think you said something that made me laugh

And I clean forgot why I'd been so upset

Grandma by Andrew Diamond

My Grandma was formidable,
A true "She who must be obeyed."
The family were in her thrall
As she ruled over one and all.
She lived five minutes walk from us
And I would visit every day,
A homage that I had to pay,
And after a respectful stay
I'd be released to go and play.
Sometimes she sent me to the shops
But never let me keep the change
And this went on from infancy
Until she died at eighty six
And I was in my latter teens.
Her funeral was magnificent,
A kind of an affair of state.
The whole world came, dressed in their best
To see my Grandma put to rest.
The family lost its matriarch
Though now, from her example,
I have become its patriarch.
And then, one night, ten years ago,
Four decades since Grandma died,
I had a very vivid dream.
She was angry, really livid
As I hadn't visited

To pay my homage as before.

So I went to the cemetery

To see what she required of me.

All the graves around her tomb

Were vandalised, smashed to the ground.

Hers was standing, quite unharmed.

No one had dared to touch her grave.

She'd, clearly, called me there to see

And now I visit regularly,

Scared to ignore her hold on me.

Margaret Griffith: In Praise of Librarians

Where we meet for our weekly writers' workshops there is a reception area, as you enter the building. It is made up of four sofas forming a square around a low Formica table. The sofas are long, low backed, thick oblong in shape, with dark blue upholstered backs and arms, and bright yellow seats, sitting on thin metal legs. They were once the height of style in the 1990s. Margaret would always arrive early for our workshops and sit there, on the same sofa, reading or catching her breath, and we would always greet her when we arrived.

When we returned from our summer break, in September 2022, there was no Margaret sat on that sofa, there was no Margaret the next week either. She wasn't answering her emails or responding to texts, which was so unlike her. Eventually we found out that Margaret had died suddenly, at the end of August.

She was our longest serving member, joining Newham Writers Workshop (NWW) in April 1990. Shortly after that she became our treasurer, a post she held until her death. She was a steadfast and solid treasurer, keeping our accounts up-to-date and making sure all subscriptions were paid. We owe our healthy financial state to her work and diligence.

Margaret worked for many years as a Librarian for Newham Public Libraries service, starting there in 1979. In 1993 she became the Assistant Cataloguer for the Housebound Readers' Service. She ran the Mobile Library, driving the van that delivered books to housebound people. She also got to know the people she delivered to, the books they liked, and provided them with conversation, even if briefly. For so many of those people, the Mobile Library was a lifeline. She worked there until she retired.

Later in life she wrote many personal essays, reflecting on the world she saw around herself. Earlier in her writing career she wrote poems and short stories that echoed her world, especially her work as a librarian, but she had a dry and yet fanciful view of that world. In 2011, NWW celebrated our 25th anniversary with a special anthology of members' work. Its title, *Bejewelled Street*, was taken from one of Margaret's poems.

Margaret loved listening to Radio 4, something she shared with many of us, she relished learning new facts and information from what she heard. We could always rely on her to know and get the obscure references some of us would slip into our writing, or recognised when one of us got that reference wrong, an in-joke backfiring on the writer, and helped us correct it. But she was no pedant, picking over every detail a writer wrote.

Her funeral was held on 9th November 2022, at East London Crematorium and Cemetery, and on that crisp winter's day so many NWW members had the chance to say goodbye to her. We had the chance to read and share her writing, her observations of life speaking for her.

It still does not feel right, to arrive for our weekly writers' workshop and not find Margaret already there, waiting in the reception area.

She is missed.

Margaret Griffith,

Born in the Republic of Ireland on 24th March 1947

and

Died in Newham, East London, on 20th August 2022

Dave Chambers & Drew Payne

The Authors' Bios

Andrew Diamond

My poems seem to write themselves and are inspired by family, life incidents and current affairs that leave a mark. I hope they amuse or get people thinking.

Belgin Durmush

I started writing short stories and poetry in the early nineties and my ambition is to one day write a novel - when I have a bit more time on my hands.

Over the years I have been inspired by Kafka and Beckett and the strange worlds they create beneath the norm, which I try to emulate in my stories.

Deadly Trivia *is a collection of my fantastical short stories, find it here*: https://tinyurl.com/4yc6euw7

Dave Chambers

I write bits and pieces of stories, and poems, mostly from my own life experiences. I'm getting on a bit, and as such if I don't finish one soon, I guess I'll never manage to be a novelist.

So I take comfort when folk talk of quality, not quantity – (that's my excuse) even if they're not talking about my stuff, so I'm working on a novella – nothing to do with the piece presented here, but something a bit shorter than a novel.

Meanwhile, I still think of the novel, but don't hold your breath . . .

Deborah Collins

She has been associated with Newham Writers since its early days in the late 1980s as Forest Gate Writers' Workshop. Born and raised in Cornwall, she has lived in Newham for 37 years and has brought up her two children in the borough while pursuing a career first in newspaper journalism and then in magazine publishing. Her main focus has been on poetry, and her self-published collection *Melon/Collie* ('a fresh, tender and sometimes funny portrait of a life that has taken in the extraordinary and the touchingly relatable, ranging from her own patch in Newham to Africa and Central America') has been much admired by the few who have read it! She has delivered performances at various venues including the Poetry Cafe in Covent Garden, UpBeat at The Gate in Forest Gate, and the Anti-Hate Festival in Southwark. She is currently putting the poetry on hold while writing a rather steamy memoir, and in semi-retirement continues to offer occasional proof-reading and editing services to those who require her professional skills.

To buy *Melon/Collie*, email: deborahjcollins@hotmail.co.uk.

Dharma Paul

I love stories in a number of media. I currently write poetry as it follows concise and distilled storytelling forms. These seem to fit how busy city life can feel.

Drew Payne

I've lived the vast majority of my life in London and worked in healthcare. Both have given me the chance to meet many different people in many different situations, which have all coloured my writing.

I am fascinated by how people live their different lives. So much of my writing tries to explore this, but it also explores issues and subjects that interest me or make me angry. Behind every headline is a story too.

I want to find the people in the situations and stories I write about.

My published books can be found here:

Amazon - https://tinyurl.com/mr3jys6s

Smashwords - https://tinyurl.com/2p9ffynw

My blog - https://drewpayne.blogspot.com/

Frances Ogiemwense

Frances is a full time Counsellor, a mother and grandmother as well as being a musician and writer.

She returned to writing during lockdown inspired by *"The Lovely Word"* writers' group based in Liverpool, and subsequently joined Newham Writers Workshop where she has received invaluable support whilst working on her latest project, "*The Oyinbo Wife*", a thriller set in Edo state Nigeria, where she holds residential status through marriage.

Frances has previously had work published by Random House and read on Radio 4.

Frank Crocker

This is my fourth year contributing to the Newham Writers Anthology, all my contributions this year are poetry. Some people have said that much of my material is just a rant, and it could be that they are right, but hey, what's the harm?

I have had my music and lyrics published, way back in time, by Acuff Rose of Nashville.

I enjoy writing lyrics, and have managed to "shoe horn" said lyrics into other writers' music, and am currently waiting for the royalties to roll in and succumb to a life of luxury and excess.

George Fuller

The police, renewable energy and the change in the materials used to build boats feature in the three poems I have published to Showtime 2023. I usually write something down soon after it happens, then months or years later I come across it by accident and it grabs my attention.

I have been a member of Newham Writers Workshop for many years now. I am glad to see that the workshop renews itself with new or returned members and some 'new' people are taking on leading roles.

I have at least three unpublished works of narrative non-fiction: a journal of months in 1993/4 spent working with other, mainly British, migrant building workers in Berlin; a journal of sailing around the estuaries of Suffolk rivers in a twelve-foot dinghy; and a story recounting working as a union member bricklayer on a Plaistow housing associations' construction project and fighting the contractor's bogus employment contract. I'd better hurry up if I am to get these published. Meanwhile, I show up at the workshop to hear other members' fascinating stories - and occasionally read a poem.

Jeff Jones

I first attended Newham Writers Worksop in 2018 with a draft of my memoirs that I had written. I had no previous experience of creative writing and before long my manuscript was transformed into a book *From Windrush to Wapping*, which is now published and for sale on Amazon, along with my second book *Once I Was Lost*. I have also taken an interest in poetry and I have written a few poems.

Find my books here:

Windrush to Wapping   - https://tinyurl.com/3d3m7y6v

Once I Was Lost - https://tinyurl.com/yemewcrm

Mandy Grainger

I've always loved reading about fearsome monsters, unlikely heroes, and morality, ever since my Dad read the Greek myths to me as a small child, along with poems by Hillaire Belloc, Edward Lear, and many others.

It wasn't until I was at university and pursuing a degree in English, however, that I established a love of creating my own stories, and with the encouragement of a respected tutor, I switched over to a joint degree and I've been honing my passion for writing ever since.

Nowadays I write in my free time with a particular interest in horror and fairy tales. I'm currently working on my first book: a supernatural mystery that pits a young boy against ghosts, witches and malevolent Gods with hidden agendas.

I write fiction mostly for escapism and to indulge my inner horror fan-girl, but my ultimate goal is to write more of the kind of against-all-odds, thrilling adventures about everyday heroes that find the strength to face their demons, that I so loved growing up. I write poetry not only as a form of entertainment, but also as a form of self-therapy. I enjoy creating poems that reflect on day-to-day life, show an appreciation for animals and nature, and that help me make sense of the world and my place in it.

Mian Obaid Shah

Mian Obaid Shah is an accomplished management consultant with a wealth of experience spanning more than 20 years in market research, consulting, and training. Alongside his professional expertise, Mr. Shah has also made significant contributions as an editor for various trade journals. His academic background includes holding an MS in International Economics from the University of Glasgow, and in addition to that he pursued additional courses, including studying at the University of Oxford.

He is the author of several books including *A Modern Approach to Applied Market Research* and *Exemplary Islamic Stories*. He also writes short stories and poetry which is being published in Magazines and anthologies. His adeptness in research has greatly benefited his creative writing endeavours, enabling him to develop richly detailed worlds and to introspectively explore his own writing practice.

His literary passion encompasses a diverse range of genres, with particular interests in historical fiction, contemporary literary realism, and speculative fiction. Mr. Shah is currently engrossed in crafting a novel centred around the journey of an Afghan refugee to the UK, delving into thought-provoking themes such as illegal immigration, racism, and the war on terrorism.

Beyond his writing pursuits, he is actively engaged in a community project with St. Paul's Cathedral. He is crafting an article focused on one of the East India Company Monuments, further showcasing his versatility and commitment to contributing to the collective knowledge and heritage.

Find his books here:

A Modern Approach to Applied Market Research - https://tinyurl.com/bddm4669

Exemplary Islamic Stories: Islamic Stories for All Ages - https://tinyurl.com/4ydkyt98

Michael Frank

I am trying to write short stories, novels and sitcoms. I have a background in marketing and teaching IT to adults. I am currently an editor and living in Pimlico. I plan to run a 10k. I like roller-blading and jazz.

Nicola Catton

I'm a new author, and published my first book in December 2022. I have lived in Newham for most of my life, was born, studied and work here. I am a qualified school teacher and worked in special education for the ten years of my twenty-year career.

I self-published my first book *The Launderette Kid* after nearly ten years of thinking about it. It's about a young boy who thinks of himself as some sort of superhero in his community. I wanted to write to encourage young writers to get writing, get creative and develop their descriptive writing skills.

The Launderette Kid, is available on Amazon, find it here: https://tinyurl.com/4bchcmf6

Paul Butler

Occasional novelist, sporadic poet, sometime dramatist, and intermittent lyricist, but with an unremitting mastery of the fine art of the unfinished.

My finished novel, *Fall of Albion*, is available on Amazon, find it here: https://tinyurl.com/3ye97kp2

Paul Germain

I'm a lifelong Newham resident with an interest in sci fi and fantasy. I was introduced to these genres as a child through TV and film. I find it easiest to write in this subject matter.

Rob Masson

I used to be a loony on the bus and not just buses but anywhere really where I had a captive audience: trains or planes and especially dentist waiting rooms. I'd go rattling on, not caring whether anyone was listening or not, on all sorts of subjects, although I did tend to specialize in conspiracy theories involving reptilian aliens among the Royal Family.

All this changed when, one day, on the Jubilee line, someone suggested that I go along to the Newham Writers Workshop. I'd probably find myself really at home, this person said. And do you know what? He was right. The only difference was that I had to write this rant about the Royal Family out on a piece of paper and read it out at one of the meetings and at the end of the year it would form a part of a collection of other rants by all the other members of this group.

So that's how I started writing short stories and I'm so busy now scribbling away that I don't have time to chatter away on buses or trains or waiting rooms. It's a funny old world, isn't it?

Ros Allison

I have been writing forever but fairly recently discovered self-publishing and have published two books so far. The only intention for my writing is entertainment, and hopefully amusement. The sort of easy light-reading you can manage after one of those days. None of my other hobbies are remotely interesting. Books are *Diary of a Foster Carer*, which is a spoof diary, and *Out of Town*, a story about a holiday that goes very wrong. Both available on Amazon as an eBook or print on demand.

I am currently working on my third book, NO HARM DONE, a cautionary tale of secrets and lies, which will be available as a print on demand or eBook later in this year.

My books on Amazon, find them here: https://tinyurl.com/3mtyf39e

Sarah Winslow

After years of travel to exotic places (Japan, Uzbekistan, Kenya etc.) where she taught English and drama at university and international school, Sarah has settled in Newham. She writes mainly poetry but also short stories, plays, sketches and occasionally has a go at a novel, time permitting in her chaotic life of acting and activism. She also drums in a samba band, rings church bells, and is a member of OW Lab Theatre. And she has a cat. Well, we all know what that means.

Afterword

If you enjoyed this anthology, why not get a copy of our previous ones, *Showtime 2022*, *Showtime 2020*, *Showtime 2019*, *Showtime 2018* and *Showtime 2017*, which are all available on **Amazon**: https://tinyurl.com/bd3dxvxy

You can also find more about us and the work by our authors at our website here:

www.newhamwriters.wordpress.com

What is Newham Writers Workshop?

We are a thriving and friendly workshop of writers ranging from novices to published authors, founded in 1986. The Workshop exists to help support what writers write, in any genre and format. Our writers write poetry, novels, drama, short stories, memoirs and songs, fiction and non-fiction.

During our term times (see our website for details), we run a weekly *Thursday night* writers workshop, and a monthly *Monday afternoon* workshop. At these workshops, writers read from their work and receive feedback from the other writers there. This feedback consists of highlighting and praising the writer on what they have done well and suggesting areas that can be improved. All critiques are supportive, we are here to help writers write what they want, not to criticise them and put them down. Many of our writers have expressed how much their writing has benefited and flourished with the workshops support. Some of the fruits of our workshops can be read in this anthology.

In addition to our workshops, we run *Termly Time Out* workshops. These are workshops led by different NWW members who share their own different and specific skills. Previous ones have included independent publishing, novel plotting, writing screenplays, narrative distance, the seven story types, sonnet writing and self-publishing on Amazon. These sessions are designed to give members extra skills to improve their writing and to access different publishing opportunities.

We have a monthly email newsletter where share what we have been doing and what we are going to do, promote member's activities and promote their work. It is also a chance to find new reading coming out of NWW. It is sent out to all members but non-members are welcome to join. To join, email us at **NewhamWriters@Hotmail.com**

New members are always welcome, whether you're new to creative writing or a seasoned veteran. You don't have to live in Newham, many of our members come from other districts of London. If you have any interest in writing, whatever genre or style, and want to develop your writing, why not try one of our workshops? It might be the start of something amazing.

Our website contains a wealth of information about us and for writers. It has details of our different writers, links to their published work, "*sharing ideas*" which is a page containing a treasure-chest of resources for writers, and there are details on becoming a member, both full and associate. Visit it here:

www.newhamwriters.wordpress.com

Contact us via our email address with any enquire, **NewhamWriters@Hotmail.com** You can ask about our workshops, enquiry about membership, give us feedback on this anthology, and join our mailing list.

You can also follow us on **Facebook**: https://tinyurl.com/mhspkbe

Printed in Great Britain
by Amazon